THE BOOK OF
BOY

CATHERINE GILBERT MURDOCK

THE BOOK OF BOY

ILLUSTRATIONS BY Ian Schoenherr

GREENWILLOW BOOKS

An Imprint of HarperCollins*Publishers*

❖ To Jill

Many thanks to the medievalist Daniel Lord Smail for reading my manuscript and for pointing out my mistakes. I fixed most of them.
—C. G. M.

The Book of Boy
Copyright © 2018 by Catherine Gilbert Murdock
Illustrations copyright © 2018 by Ian Schoenherr

The text of this book is set in 11-point HoeflerText.
Book design by Paul Zakris

Library of Congress Cataloging-in-Publication Data

Names: Murdock, Catherine Gilbert, author. | Schoenherr, Ian, illustrator.
Title: The book of Boy / by Catherine Gilbert Murdock ; illustrations by Ian Schoenherr.
Description: First edition. | New York, NY : Greenwillow Books, an imprint of HarperCollinsPublishers, [2018] | Summary: In 1350, a boy with a large hump on his back becomes the servant of a shadowy pilgrim on his way to Rome, who pulls the boy into a dangerous expedition across Europe to gather the seven precious relics of Saint Peter.
Identifiers: LCCN 2017043536 | ISBN 9780062686206 (hardback)
Subjects: | CYAC: Relics—Fiction. | Pilgrims and pilgrimages—Fiction. | Adventure and adventurers—Fiction. | Voyages and travels—Fiction. | People with disabilities—Fiction. | Middle Ages—Fiction. | BISAC: JUVENILE FICTION / Historical / Medieval. | JUVENILE FICTION / Action & Adventure / General. | JUVENILE FICTION / Social Issues / Self-Esteem & Self-Reliance.
Classification: LCC PZ7.M9416 Bo 2018 | DDC [Fic]—dc23 LC record available at https://lccn.loc.gov/2017043536

18 19 20 21 22 CG/LSCH 10 9 8 7 6 5 4
First Edition

 Greenwillow Books

The key to hell picks all locks

∙⋮∙

CONTENTS

Part I: Departure

Part II: The Relic Thief

Part III: Deceit and Calamity and Ruin

Part IV: Arrival

I

Departure

1 ⋮ The Stranger

This story, like another, begins with an apple. The apple in my tale was not ripe and tempting but wrinkled and old, too high to pluck and too stubborn to drop. It hung from a whip-thin branch, dancing in the cold March wind. The goats pranced around the tree trunk, bleating their frustration.

"Do not be so greedy, goats," I called as I climbed. "You are so much like pigs that Cook will carve you into hams!" But I laughed as I scolded to lighten the threat. The branches clawed this way and that, for the orchard had not been pruned in two years, and the shoots were as tangled as bird nests. "Stop scratching me, tree," I whispered. "I will not hurt you. I promise." The apple tree was higher than I had supposed, but I am not feared of heights and I am not feared of climbing—*you could climb a cloud,* Father Petrus used to say, may God rest his soul. *You're a miracle, Boy,* he would add, so often that I almost believed him.

Up I climbed, till my head was as high as the orchard. I could see the manor, guarding us from wicked men. "Goats," I called, "I can see our shed!"

'Twas then I glimpsed the pilgrim. The goats could not see him because the ditches also had run wild these past two years. "He is tall, goats, and wears a brown pilgrim robe and cloak and wide hat, with a staff as tall as he, and he carries a pack on a long pole. Perhaps he journeys to the Holy Land, or to Rome to see the key to heaven." I marveled at a soul so fortunate as to travel the earth whilst seeking God's favor, and I waved. But the pilgrim did not wave back.

So I resolved to impress him. I walked along one branch and another without even holding a twig, for pride is the downfall of every soul. Closer I stepped to that apple . . . I leaped and snatched it, and I fell through the chill March air, but I am not feared of falling, and I tumbled on the cold ground with leaves on my hood and a laugh on my lips. Naught in the world is so joyous as the feeling of flight.

The goats pushed in: *bah!* they snorted. *You should jump less and feed us more.* The brown nanny snatched the apple from my fist and dashed off, her eyes gleaming with gluttony, for goats know well the vices.

I lay giggling at life and the goats and the bright cold day. 'Twould not be cold forever, and soon enough the apple blossoms would swell as life swelled already in the bellies of the goats. . . .

The pilgrim loomed over me, the brim of his hat blocking the sky.

Oh, he startled me. This was my orchard, a place for me and the goats.

"Who's your master?" The pilgrim's face was shadowed, his voice dark.

He did not even greet me. Should I greet him? Was it my place to?

"Do you speak?"

"Y-yes."

"Where would your master be?"

I scrambled to my feet, brushing dead grass off my hood and goatskin and hose. The pilgrim had a dozen pilgrim badges pinned to his hat: the shell of Saint James, the head of Saint Thomas . . . goodness but this man had traveled far.

I pointed across the weed-choked ditch toward the manor. "There."

"Hmph." He turned, staff in hand, and started off. "Well? Take me there."

"Oh! Yes . . . milord." I should add *milord,* to be polite.

"And stand up straight."

My cheeks flushed. Why did he notice? Why did everyone notice? "I am," I whispered.

"Hmph. A hunchback. You can walk at least." He snapped his fingers at the pack he had been carrying, the pack on the end of the pole. "Bring that for me. And careful: 'tis worth more than you are."

I hurried for the pack, unsure whether to hold it in my arms—was it truly worth more than me?—or to balance the pole on my shoulder as the pilgrim had. The goats gathered around, but I held the pack out of reach. No telling what a goat might do.

I set off after the pilgrim, keeping my head down. Everyone's a hunchback when they hunch.

He strode toward the manor, not asking the route, but he did not need to, for the goats had marked the path in their way. I followed, the pole tangling in my legs. He moved so fast I had to trot.

"What do they call you?"

I sensed him staring at me, and wished he wouldn't. "Boy."

He snorted. "What does your mother call you?"

"Haven't got a mother."

"Ah. Pestilence."

"Never had one."

"Never?" he asked mockingly.

I shook my head. Father Petrus hadn't been a mother, though he'd come close. He was the one who named me Boy. *Never reveal yourself, Boy.* . . . He hit me when he spoke this, to make certain I minded.

"What of your father?"

I shrugged. The manor had more than one child without a pa.

Beneath the wide brim of his hat, his eyes caught the light. "Ah. The face of an angel and body of a fiend—I suppose that defines a boy right enough."

"Not *a* boy. *Boy.* That's my name." I did not care for the words he tossed about. I did not care for people calling me anything other than Boy.

We passed the huts, or what was left of them. The pilgrim walked straight, not following the swerve in the trail, for even the goats avoided the huts.

In the first hut—now a blackened scar full of two years' weeds—had lived a shepherd, God rest his soul, who played a pipe. He had promised to teach me, but pestilence took him away before he could. Perhaps he lived now in paradise, piping.

The second hut once held a widow and her son. They perished, too, the both of them. They went to sleep but never did they awaken, and their hut was now only four charred posts. *Please,* I prayed. *Heavenly saints, see them into paradise.*

I crept past the final hut, its thatch rotting and doorway dark. No one had been left to burn it. In that place lived the family that called me a monster, even the smallest who barely could talk, and the mother laughed when her children threw stones.

I tried to pray for them as I passed, but the words would not form in my mind. My fingers reached beneath my hood for the scar on my scalp. *May God forgive my absence of mercy.*

"Both hands with that pack, Boy," the pilgrim ordered, his boots crunching on the frosty grass.

Quick I snatched my hand back. I did not like this pilgrim. I did not like a man who saw what he needn't and did not fear what he should. This pilgrim man was dangerous.

2 ∵ Sold for a Prayer

The pilgrim broke a path through the ditch. I hurried after him, the goats close behind me, for the ditch had been known to shelter wolves.

There stood the manor on its hill, vineyards draped around it like a fine lady's skirts. "Sir Jacques is there." I pointed. "Milord."

"Take me to him."

"But—" What to say? I swallowed. "Yes, milord."

The goats held back as we climbed the hill. We were none of us welcome at the manor—I because of my hump, and the goats because they irked the dogs. We had been welcome once, for milady enjoyed the goats' spunk and my service, but milady was gone now, milady and her three sweet babies, and another woman made the rules.

The dogs ran up when I entered the courtyard; we were great friends, the dogs and I. They kept their distance from the pilgrim, however, for dogs are wise to strangers. I hunched inside the wagging circle, holding the pilgrim's pack away from their curious noses. Keeping an eye out for stones.

Sir Jacques sat in the sunny spot to which he was carried whenever the day was fresh enough to release him from the stink of his bed. No matter how the servants fussed—no matter how milady had fussed whilst she lived—Sir Jacques refused to wear a cap. Perhaps the cloth chafed, or perhaps what was left of his mind wanted the world to see his suffering. From across the courtyard I could see the dent in his skull—the dent kicked into his head on the day of that fateful joust. He stared at naught, drooling.

"Ah," said the pilgrim. "Your master."

I nodded, relieved I would not need to explain.

The dogs sniffed at the pilgrim, their noses twitching. Now I could smell it, drifting through the cold air: a sour scent I did not care for.

A voice screeched toward us: "I will slap you blind if I see you wasting good eggs. . . . Who's this?" Cook came to the kitchen door, wiping her hands on a gown. Milady's, that gown had been, though the seams were now let out and sour milk stained the cuffs.

The pilgrim bowed his head but—I noticed—did not remove his hat. "Good morning, madam. I am Secundus, a humble pilgrim." The word *humble* twisted in his mouth and came out crooked.

The dogs buried their heads under my elbows: *Boy, Boy, we don't like that man, Boy.*

"I've no donations for pilgrims," Cook snapped. "Find your bread at a public house as the law allows." She knew her law, Cook did.

Secundus smiled a smile that was no smile at all. "I pilgrim to the feast day of Saint-Peter's-Step."

Saint-Peter's-Step? Saint-Peter's-Step was a great town three days away! The lame journeyed there seeking miracles. Sideways I studied the sour-smelling pilgrim. He did not look lame.

"What of it?" growled Cook.

His eyes gleamed. "I should like this lad to accompany me. This boy who climbs so well."

The pilgrim wanted me? Me? To travel three days away?

Boy, Boy, that man scares us, he does, the dogs whispered.

He scares me, too, I whispered back.

"Boy?" Cook scoffed. "He's useless." She'd called me worse names, she had. She'd said more than once that my monster hump had brought the pestilence upon us.

Secundus gestured to the pack in my arms. "My parcel burdens me. I would he carried it."

The pack had no weight at all! Naught he said rang true. Pilgrim he might be, but this man had sin stitched into his soul.

Cook's eyebrows rose. "A servant you're wanting? Well, I'll need payment for his absence. Someone must care for the goats."

"If he is as useless as you claim, he will not be missed."

Cook frowned. She did not like her own words used against her.

"A child so young, so innocent . . ." The pilgrim sighed. "The merciful Church allows him to pray for another in his stead—and a feast-day prayer carries special virtue. Tell me, dear woman: do you know anyone who might be in need of a blessing? A sinner seeking relief from the fires of eternal damnation?"

Cook's lips went white. She glared at Secundus, and at me, and she could not help but look over at Sir Jacques so helpless and drooling—her master till she made him her husband.

How did the pilgrim know?

"A prayer and a donation, of course." Secundus smiled a cold smile.

Cook stomped back into the kitchen.

The pilgrim tapped his fingers against his staff, his nails clicking on the wood, not at all flustered by Cook's snapping and growling and stomping. I hunched beside him, my mind a whirl. One two three days to Saint-Peter's-Step, and one two three back. That made one two three four five six days. How would I survive six days with this man?

Boy, Boy, what is happening? the dogs asked. *We're worried, Boy, Boy!*

I scratched their ears. *You're not the ones who should worry.*

"Two hands on that pack, Boy."

The pilgrim seemed to see everything. I gripped the pack, shivering.

Cook hustled out with a silver cup engraved with a stag: Sir Jacques's toasting cup when he yet could speak. She jammed the cup into my hands. "My donation. Don't let *him*"—gesturing to the pilgrim—"do naught with it. Not sell it or touch it or use it himself. Pray for Sir Jacques, Boy. Pray for our king, the good king of France. And pray . . ."

I looked at her. *Tell me, Cook. Tell me the words I should say so God forgives you.* I did not speak these words, but perhaps she saw them on my face. She'd seen them before.

"Pray for me," she said, not meeting my eyes. She flicked her skirts—milady's skirts. Milady, who now burned in torment because Cook had not sent for a priest. "Promise you will."

"I promise," I vowed. Cook was not someone to be on the wrong side of.

"And," Secundus added, "a coin for our journey? We must eat."

"Boy don't eat."

"I do. And then I will see him to the altar to pray for your soul."

Fire danced from Cook's eyes. . . . With a hiss, she tossed a coin to the pilgrim.

How did he know?

He slipped the coin into his purse. "Come, Boy. We have leagues to travel."

I looked at Cook: "Please . . ." That is how frightened I was: I would admit it even to her.

But Cook only glared; her sharp eyes looked me up and down, and looked up and down the pilgrim, calculating the value of the badges pinned to his hat, and of his worn leather boots. "I'll want to hear every detail. Now if you'll excuse me, pilgrim, I've many tasks waiting." She slammed the door in my face, and in the face of the pilgrim. Still I could hear her through the walls: "Did you attend to the bread? I see you didn't. . . ."

I must obey Cook. Cook, who saw all and who never stopped tallying. Who judged that a silver cup would buy her entrance to heaven. I must follow this man and do as he told me. 'Twould only be six days. I could manage that many days, perhaps, if I was brave.

Secundus was halfway across the courtyard—goodness, he moved fast. I hurried after him, the dogs loping beside me.

Too late I heard a heavy step. A shadow fell across the cattle shed door.

The dogs melted away.

"Well, look who's here," sneered Ox. Only a few years older than me, he was, but man-sized, with a man's voice.

I ducked, and though I gripped the cup and Secundus's pack and his pole, my fingers still reached for the scar beneath my eye. The big scar. It had bled for days.

"Monster's made himself somebody's pet," purred Ox, for though Ox was as big as a bear and as dumb as a boulder, he was cruel as a boar, and I was his favorite prey.

The pilgrim stopped, studying Ox chuckling at his own jest, and motioned for him to approach.

Ox's chuckle faded, and his small eyes darted about. He had no choice but to shuffle forward.

All this I watched like a mouse trapped with two vipers.

Ox was big, but he was not tall. Not as tall as Secundus. Not as . . . scary.

Quick as a slap Secundus moved, jamming his staff under Ox's jaw. Ox's head snapped up, and he stared with shocked wide eyes.

My head came up, too. Never had I seen someone take on Ox.

"You strike me as a sinner." Secundus spoke quietly. "Do you protect the weak, or the strong?"

Ox licked his lips. "I . . . I dunno."

Secundus waited. I waited, biting my cheeks in fear. The sun held its place in the sky.

Ox's eyes darted in my direction. "Mebbe I . . . don't."

"Don't do what?"

"P-protect the weak."

"Ah." Secundus smiled a smile of ice. "Then you are most definitely a sinner." He paused. "Do you know what happens to those who do not protect the weak?"

Ox tried to swallow.

"They go to hell." The pilgrim's breath steamed in the cold air. He leaned close, his voice quiet. "Shall I tell you what hell is like?"

With the smallest of gestures Ox shook his head.

Secundus stepped back.

Ox collapsed like a broken puppet.

"Come, Boy. Leagues to walk."

Ox clutched his throat, his eyes on the pilgrim. He did not call me a monster. He did not throw stones.

I hurried after Secundus. This pilgrim scared me, he did. But at least he did not call me names. He did not throw stones. In fact, he challenged the stone throwers. He'd frightened the worst stone thrower of them all, so much that great big Ox collapsed like a broken puppet.

He had power, this pilgrim. And already his power was touching me. Transforming me as a rotten apple infects its neighbors.

I should have kept my eyes forward, I knew. But as I left the courtyard, I turned back to Ox and did something I had never once in my life dared to do.

I stuck out my tongue.

3 ⫶ Rib Tooth Thumb Shin Dust Skull Tomb

No sooner was I descending the hill, clutching cup and pack and pole, than I regretted my gesture. Ox had a small mind but a long memory. Six days was not enough for him to forget.

The goats trailed us, bleating. "Go!" barked Secundus. "Off with you."

They glared at him. He glared back and shook his staff.

Go, goats, I told them. *I will return in six days.*

Bah, they snorted. *Who will entertain us whilst you're gone?*

I could not but smile. *You will have to entertain yourselves.*

Bah. That's not an answer. One by one, however, they trotted off, flicking their tails.

Good-bye, goats. May the saints keep you safe.

Bah! You silly creature: of course we'll be safe. We're goats.

And so I was alone, following the pilgrim. I must be ready to obey, or flee. . . .

The manor grew small behind me, then disappeared behind weeds. Those weeds should be cut, they should. Sir Jacques would never allow such disorder—

Secundus halted, hand out. "Give me the cup."

I should not let him touch it. Cook ordered me so.

His eyebrows rose. "I said give me the cup, Boy."

Ever so reluctantly, I passed him Sir Jacques's treasure. How weak I was.

The cup disappeared into a pocket in his robe. Out came a length of cord. "Hold the pack on your back," he ordered. Right quick he tied the pack over my hump and shaggy goat-skin. He did not, I noticed, touch the pack. "If you try to open this, I will see you hanged." He said this as he said all his words, to the air and not to me. "Also if you run away."

I shivered.

"'Tis good you are scared. Fear will make you careful." He tested the knots on my chest, then recommenced walking. "Put that pole to use as a walking stick. And hurry."

I did as I was told, reluctant at first, but the pole developed into a sweet-tempered companion, and my pace quickened with a stick to aid me. The cords pulled across my chest, but the pack felt gentler than I would have imagined. Indeed, it warmed my hump, even through the goatskin I wore.

We reached the crossroads. The pilgrim paused.

"Saint-Peter's-Step is this way," I offered, pointing straight. "And that road"—I pointed right—"goes all the way to a sea that tastes of salt. A traveler told me so."

"Is that a fact?" he asked with an odd smile so that I decided 'twas wisest not to speak more.

We came to the field of Michel the plowman. After pestilence took his son, Michel gave me his son's boots, which were the boots I wore now, stuffed with wool so they fit me, and his son's hose that I held up with string, and his red hood so my head should never be cold. Then Michel left because the manor held naught but sadness for him, and now his field was empty.

We came to the furthest place I had ever been: a beech tree broader than two men. Three years back, before the pestilence, Sir Jacques had ridden off to a tourney, and milady wanted to see him well fêted when he returned. So she gave me a flask of wine and sent me all the way to this tree to greet him. The sun crossed the sky till I grew right fearful, but at last he appeared with a token and a bag of coins because he always won till his very last tourney, and he lifted me onto his charger so that I might ride with him back to the manor. And he told me his horse had never been so calm as with me upon him, and perchance I should switch from goats to horses because a boy who can calm a horse is worth the price of five good dogs.

We passed the beech tree, the pilgrim and I, and then I was walking on a road I did not know, but my head was so full of memories that my fear had to move over like a child on a bench and make room.

All day the pilgrim strode, and I did my best to keep up. We passed empty villages where doorways gaped like mouths without teeth, and dark tangles of weeds where wicked things might hide, and glad I was to hurry. As the sun settled, our shadows stretched before us. Still the pilgrim did not stop.

"Milord?" I whispered, my voice trembling, and my legs. He coughed but did not answer.

At last we came to a clearing marked with a circle of ashes. Secundus peered about, and nodded to himself, and dropped his staff and hat.

"We sleep here?" I could not keep the fear from my voice. What if outlaws found us, or brigands, or wolves? I shivered at the thought of the darkness surrounding us, and glint-eyed wolves creeping through the night. . . .

"It would appear so." He stepped into the bushes. I followed. "Can a man have no privacy?" he snapped, and I scuttled away, though not far. I, too, squatted as men do, trying not to be fearful.

The pilgrim offered me dried meat from his purse, which I took because I must accept food when it's offered, though I took only a small piece so as not to waste it. He set to work building a fire.

I wished I could sit near him because the ground was so cold and the dark so frightening. But I was feared to approach. I thought of removing the pack tied to my back, but I was feared to ask permission, and in truth the pack warmed me, which was a comfort. I said my prayers, praying for poor Sir Jacques who had lost his mind to the kick of a horse, and for the souls of milady and her three sweet babies, and for Father Petrus whom God had taken before pestilence came. I prayed that Ox would forget I'd stuck out my tongue. I prayed wolves would not find me. I did not pray for Cook—I'd pray for her at Saint-Peter's-Step.

I curled up with my hose and goatskin, and pulled my hood close around my neck. The fire was barely more than kindling, but still I held my hands to its warmth.

Secundus produced a book. A book! A small book, quite battered with scuffs and grime. The edges were black as though they'd been burned. The book too stank sour.

"You can read, milord?"

"Ah. Yes. 'Tis a liability of my occupation."

"Of pilgriming?"

He barked a laugh. "I once was a lawyer."

I did not say anything because I was so amazed to meet a man who could read, which even Father Petrus could not do, and also I did not know that word.

"I studied law—you know laws? I advised men." He stared at the fire. "Very powerful men."

"And now you go on pilgrimage." I should say something, I felt.

"Ah. Yes. I am on a quest, Boy. A quest for seven objects. Seven relics as precious as anything on this earth. Seven relics that will save me." He held the book so I could see a page of writing. "Rib tooth thumb shin," he recited. "Dust skull tomb."

"Rib tooth thumb shin dust skull home," I whispered to myself. How grand these words sounded. Like a prayer.

"Tooth is my next task, and challenging it will be. But I am more optimistic, now that I have a boy who can climb." He slipped the book into his robe. "The first task I've already accomplished. Do you know the story of Peter, Boy?"

"Of Saint Peter?" Indeed I did, from Father Petrus. "Peter was a simple fisherman but he became the very first pope of Rome, and now he minds the gates of heaven."

The pilgrim nodded. "You've been taught well. Guard that pack, Boy. Guard it as you would your life. For within that pack rests one of Saint Peter's ribs."

4 ∴ Pestilence

Curled in the crook of a tree: that is my second memory. Curled and scared, for boys surrounded the tree and threw stones. "We caught a monster," they cried, and shouted that the priest would soon arrive to destroy me. I ducked the stones as best I could, and covered my face with my hands, and I wept.

A red-faced old man came puffing up, leaning on his stick to catch his breath. A boy cocked his arm to throw a stone, and Father Petrus thwacked him—the father was keen on thwacking, he was—and informed the boys that they were as stupid as fleas. He sent them away and settled himself, muttering.

I crept from the tree so that I might better listen. The old man spoke to me, and offered a blanket as I had no clothes, and took me to his room behind the church, and let me sweep for him and run his errands, and taught me the words of his muttering, which turned out to be prayers.

He knew of my hump and my secrets. "Never reveal yourself!" he would thunder, and when I chanced to remove my tunic due to itching or heat, he'd thwack me till I knew in my marrow that I must never reveal myself, not even in bed when all good men sleep naked. I must never show myself nor touch my hump for my hump was wicked and made me a monster—that, and my other secret. When folk commented on my hump or my monstrousness, he thwacked them.

So Father Petrus tended to me and clothed me and showed me his name Petrus *in the Bible, for he knew those letters at least. I cared for him greatly, and even when I served Sir Jacques and milady, still I brought him goat's milk that he loved, till he died, but such is God's grace that He took Father Petrus before the pestilence so the kind priest would not know that horror.*

That is my second memory, and all the other memories that grew from it. But my first memory is of sleeping in a flock of doves, soft warm wings all about me, and murmuring, and darkness. Only this time the doves were pecking. Gently at first, and then ouch—

"What is the meaning of this!"

Sharpness woke me—sharp words in my ears and a sharp

poke in my ribs. I blinked at the bright light filling the goat shed, and the sounds I had never heard a goat speak.

But wait—I was not in the goat shed at all. I was outside, in a forest. Around me goats curled, bleating. Again I was poked—a staff, a man . . . Secundus.

At once I was awake, struggling to free myself from this strange pile of goats.

"You brought them here?" he asked, furious.

These were goats, yes, but their coats were matted with brambles, and the pack included a billy with great horns and a glorious stink. Naught stinks quite like a billy goat.

"N-no, milord."

"They simply appeared in the night?"

"These are not my goats."

"Hmph," said Secundus.

The biggest nanny glared at him. She was missing half a horn and looked to be tougher than flint. She hauled herself upright and passed a great stream of water that steamed on the cold ground.

Secundus watched, his mouth twisting. He turned away. "Is my pack secure?"

"Yes, milord." Last night's conversation flooded my mind. I carried a rib of Saint Peter, the first pope of Rome—me, a humble goatherd!

"Come, Boy." He strode away. The goats trotted in the other direction.

Good-bye, goats. Thank you for warming me. I shuddered to think how I would have survived the chilled night without them. If I would have survived.

They flicked their tails: *Bah. We do not think much of your master.* Goats never think much of people.

Secundus offered me a drink from his flask but I said no thank you, for flask water tastes right awful, though I took a piece of meat because I must accept food when it's offered. I said my prayers, praying that God forgive me for praying on foot, but tarrying did not sit well with this pilgrim.

I prayed for milady and Sir Jacques as always, and Father Petrus, and I added a prayer to Saint Peter, thanking him for letting me bear him. No wonder the pack warmed me so. *Rib tooth thumb thumb thumb thumb home* . . . No, that was not it. *Rib tooth thumb something something something home* . . . Well, seven relics there were, even if I could not remember them all. And I bore the rib upon my back!

All that morning we walked, rabbits dashing away. The crows warned the forest of our presence, and foxes screamed. Once I heard the howl of a wolf, which sent my heart beating, but I did not hear it again.

The trees thinned out, and praise Saint Peter, we were back in the land of man.

"Do you ever talk?"

I jumped. "Me?"

"No, I am addressing that puddle.... Of course I mean you."

"Oh. Yes, milord." I could sense him studying me.

"Tell me of your master, Boy, for I suspect it is a story worth hearing."

"Sir Jacques? The story is terribly sad."

"I do not doubt. But the road is long, and words are sometimes better than silence."

"Yes, milord." I pondered. "Sir Jacques is—was—a great fighter, and went to war when the English invaded French lands, and the good king of France rewarded him with the manor you saw. Sir Jacques was a fine master but fighting never left his blood, and he could not bear mention of a tournament but that he should go and best other men as he'd bested the English. He brought back many a token and many a purse, and one day he brought back milady, who was pious and kind and who taught me to serve and cut my hair. She begged Sir Jacques to stop jousting, and begged him all the more after his son was born, and two little daughters. But Sir Jacques said he was not a farmer and went off on his great black charger." *Which once I rode to the manor with Sir Jacques himself,* I added to myself, remembering that glorious day.

"Yes?" Secundus prodded.

"So . . . so all was right with the world till two springs ago when Sir Jacques rode off but did not come back, and did not come back the next day, either, so that milady wept with worry and held her babies close. On the third day Sir Jacques returned. He returned lying in a wagon, which a knight never would do. A horse had kicked his helmet and sent a piece of iron right into his skull. A priest administered last rites because everyone knew he'd soon perish. But he did not." I paused. "Instead other men sickened with black sores where their limbs met their bodies, and the stableboys, and the three sweet babies still with their milk teeth. Milady tended to them till she sickened, too, and then . . . they died. Many people died."

"Many people died. Yes." He sighed. "But not Sir Jacques. Not the cook."

"No. But her name is no longer Cook. Now people call her milady because the first milady is gone."

"Ah. So this knight has a wife who is not noble born. I figured that was her sin."

"No!" How odd he should think that. Every soul needs a mate—Father Petrus said so. Cook had not sinned by marrying Sir Jacques. Indeed, some greedy nobleman would have claimed the manor had she not wed him, what with all his uncles perished. . . . I pondered, frowning. Memories bubbled inside me like bad dreams. "Milord?"

"Ah. You still have a tongue."

"When milady sickened, she begged for a priest so that she might confess before she died."

"Ah. But your cook did not send for the priest."

"No." I began to weep. "Milady did not have last rites. So now she burns in hell!"

"Hmph. Dry your eyes, Boy," he ordered, his voice hard. "Your precious lady is not there."

My head came up. "Truly, milord?"

"I vow it on my—" His face was grim. "I vow it on my life. Hell is for sinners. Believe me."

"But she did not confess—"

"What of it? That woman could in no way be a sinner." His face softened. "She cut your hair."

And so gladness touched my heart because this man who knew so much promised that milady was safe. But my spirits sank, too, for this talk of pestilence had opened a door within my mind, and all manner of memories flooded out. Memories of people now passed. *Be kind to them, Saint Peter. Please take them into paradise.*

Secundus was as lost in his thoughts as I in mine, his face solemn. He did not respond when a plowman called a greeting—he did not even nod. When we came to a crossroad marked with a pile of stones, he pulled out his book to study it, and led us off to the right. He studied his book again when we crested a hill, and before us spread green hills and plowed valleys, and snow-covered mountains. He peered at the view, and turned his book to examine a drawing, but even as he nodded he frowned.

We came upon an orchard, the trees as wild and unpruned as the orchard back home; it looked like a field filled with madmen. Poor trees. Folk had died in this place too. . . .

Words are sometimes better than silence, Secundus said. But I could think of no words to say, for my memories of the dead took all the life from me.

In silence we strode till dusk overtook us.

5 ∴ The Stone Bridge

We came to a hayfield with a haystack yet left from winter, and there Secundus made camp, on the lee side out of the wind. He built a small fire, and by its flickering light studied his wee stinky book. "Saint-Peter's-Step possesses a relic of great value," he said, more to himself. "It is guarded, every minute."

"The tooth?"

He looked up. "What did you say?"

"The tooth. 'Rib tooth thumb something something something home.' I'm sorry; I can't remember."

"You have a quicker mind than I supposed. Yes, the tooth: rib tooth thumb shin dust skull tomb. But I need something else first." He tapped his book. "I happen to know that on the day of the feast of Saint-Peter's-Step, a party of monks will attempt to steal the town's relic."

"No!"

"Yes, sadly. A monk from the monastery of Saint-Peter's-Mount told me this only a short time ago. He was quite . . . distressed. You and I must protect it."

"I shall, milord. I shall protect it as I protect the rib of Saint Peter!"

"What a companion I have found. . . ." He settled himself into the hay. "Do you want to hear the story of the rib?"

"Oh, please, yes." Everyone likes a good story.

He poked at the fire. "I have traveled a long way, Boy. For a very long time. At last I arrived in Paris—"

"You've been to Paris, milord?"

"Yes, Boy."

"You traveled all the way from Paris to here?"

"Yes. May I continue? I arrived in Paris very tired—tired, and overwhelmed. 'Twas so unlike the place I'd left. The smells. The cold. To my fortune, the king was away."

"The king of France?" I could not help myself.

"The king of France. I saw his palace, which is in the style of barbarians—the whole city is. The whole world. No one respects proportion or order. All that is beautiful has been lost. . . ." With effort he composed himself. "So. I found the palace. I found the holy chapel within, where the kings of France store their most valued relics. And it—never have I been more surprised—the chapel was lovely. In the style of barbarians, and yet . . . Moonlight streaming through the chapel's walls—walls of colored glass. 'Twas like standing in the heart of a jewel."

"The heart of a jewel," I whispered. . . . How marvelous.

"So many relics—a kingdom's worth. But I cared only for one. Which I located easily enough. It was small, a mere fragment of rib. But then . . ." His voice grew rough. "I discovered a terrible truth—a truth for which I'd had no warning whatsoever." He held up his hand, and in the firelight I could see a shiny scar on his palm—a recent burn.

"The relic *marked* you?" My eyes went wide.

"For so long I heard twaddle about the power of relics. But I never believed it." He rubbed his palm. "Not till now."

"Does the rib burn everyone?" Might it burn me?

"No." His eyes glittered in the firelight. "So I fashioned myself a pack to hold the rib I could not touch, and I found a stick to carry the pack, and I made my way south. And that is the tale of the rib."

What a fine tale it was. To stand in the heart of a jewel, with a kingdom's worth of relics. To see—to know—the rib of Saint Peter. I smiled, curled in the moldy hay. Some folk the rib burned, it seemed, and other folk it warmed.

That night I dreamed of Saint Peter at the gates of paradise, thanking me for his rib. The gates were warm, and Saint Peter was warm, though he smelled odd. The gates were soggy, somehow. . . .

I awoke to the stink of wet wool, and a half-dozen sheep nestled around me.

"Boy?" came a voice, though I could not see Secundus for the pile of sheep. 'Twas like being smothered by a wet smelly cloud.

I struggled my way out of the flock, the sheep bleating their annoyance. The poor creatures had not been shorn since the pestilence, and mist beaded on their shaggy coats, and they watched with bland eyes as we departed.

I accepted some cheese from Secundus, though cheese is only rotten milk, and put my lips to his flask, and made sure his pack was secure on my hump, the pack with the rib of Saint Peter.

All day we hurried under low clouds, the air filled with the smells of wet fields. We traveled through a village where barking dogs made sure we did not linger, though several wagged their tails, which shows that even dogs can be liars, and when I told them my name they trailed us repeating *Boy, Boy, Boy!* till we were away.

Our road joined another. We came upon a laborer with a large bundle on his back: a bundle that turned out to be an old man with a crippled foot.

"Ye cannot manage a single step without jostling," the old man was shouting. "You are the slowest creature since Satan fell from heaven. . . . Ho there, pilgrim," he called to Secundus. "Walk with us. Perhaps your pace will inspire this worthless son of mine."

Were my son to carry me, thought I, *I should thank him with every step.*

The old man pointed to his leg twisted sideways. "I've a bad foot, you know. I go to Saint-Peter's-Step to be cured. The town has a relic stored in a great strong chest, but on feast days the good priests reveal it so that all who come may know its blessings."

"So I have heard," murmured Secundus.

I glanced at Secundus. Would he mention that we were protecting the relic? Apparently not.

In due course the old man—having chided his son for jostling, and the clouds for drizzling, and Secundus and me for dullness—said he needed to rest, and Secundus begged our leave.

"I declare," Secundus whispered to me, "pilgriming would be the world's greatest pursuit were it not for other pilgrims."

I giggled because it was true and because jesting is joyous, even in drizzle.

At that moment a thought struck me: the old man had said not a word about me! He had not called me hunchback or monster, and neither he nor his son made any sign of protection. It could not be kindness, no, for the old man did not strike me as kind. It must be they did not notice.

So stunned was I that I reached for my hump, which was wrong for I never must touch it, but curiosity overwhelmed sense. The hump was there same as always, with the pack atop it like the shell of a beetle. . . .

The pack hid my hump. The pack with the rib of Saint Peter.

Would the pack hide my hump from other folk's eyes? Now I could not wait for more people!

We came upon a traveler and then several, pilgrims and merchants and cripples, men and women and boys and girls, all heading to the feast day of Saint-Peter's-Step. They nodded as we passed, or spoke. But not one made the sign of protection. A party of ten pilgrims drank from a small barrel they carried, yet even they did not curse or taunt me, and well do I know how wine fuels taunting.

With each passing stranger, I stood taller. *To that soul,* I would think, *I am only a boy. A boy and a servant and naught else.* And so though our travel worsened as people and oxen churned the road into muck, my steps grew lighter. *Thank you, Saint Peter, for hiding my hump.*

We passed a bend in the road, and there appeared a town grander than anything I had ever known, with a forest of smoking chimneys and a wall wrapped like a bandage around its outside, and a great stone bridge so long that I could not throw a pebble its length. Guards stood at the bridge's near end, and every soul who passed had to hand them a coin, or some other payment for coins are hard to come by.

"Ah. Tollmen," murmured Secundus, and a woman with a basket of piglets laughed a bitter laugh, and over their squeals she asked the Good Lord to inflict tollmen with what they deserved.

The crowd pressed hard and restless toward the bridge but the tollmen would take their time, and whilst others minded I did not, because in one two three four days I would be home again, and would have the rest of my life to recall this.

A vintner argued that his wine was not worth being taxed, that indeed it would sicken them, but the tollmen shook their heads and took a cup of his wine as their coin. A farmwife led a gaggle of geese up to the bridge, all of them hissing as she paid eggs to the tollmen.

Before us walked three nuns in gray habits, their heads together against the sins of the world. "The holy orders pay no tax," the first nun announced to the tollmen.

The tollman peered at them, for the nuns shuffled and hunched in a queer manner. At that minute the habit of the second nun quite erupted, and out flopped a rooster with an angry screech, causing everyone to jump, even the nuns and most especially the tollmen, who had not expected the sisters to be smuggling a fowl.

Oh, the crowd laughed.

"I had no idea—" began the second nun as the first nun cried, "We owe no tax if we haven't the bird!" And indeed they did not, for the rooster flapped away, crowing that he had evaded the nuns and the tax and the chopping block.

Then 'twas our turn, Secundus and me, the crowd still chuckling. "Are ye a real pilgrim?" one tollman asked Secundus. The other tollman looked me over but his expression did not change, and he paid no notice of my hump beneath the pack of Saint Peter.

"My boy carries our food," Secundus answered, coughing, "and I a humble offering for the altar. Surely you have plumper birds to pluck"—which again set the crowd to laughing.

The tollmen motioned us through, and so we crossed the bridge.

Behold: I was walking over water deeper than men. Oh, the genius of God and masons. "Milord? Should we not warn the townsfolk that monks will try to steal their relic?"

"That is not our task, Boy. Our task is to keep it safe."

6 ❖ Saint-Peter's-Step

Saint-Peter's-Step! Thick was the crowd and thick the stench, of people and smoke and everything else. Here was a lady with a white mule and three servants; there a troupe of pilgrims in prayer; here a housewife selling wine from her doorstep; there beggars with crippled legs but lusty voices. My stick tripped one person and another, so I crept along not knowing where to squirm. And then I lost Secundus.

By the goodness of heaven I lost him for only a minute, but oh, how my heart pounded in that one minute's time. "Secundus," I screamed, but my voice could not pierce the din, and the crowd pressed in, and everyone, it seemed, wore pilgrim garb.

Secundus appeared, his face tight with anger, and lifted his hand so I thought he would strike me. But instead he reached into his robe for a length of rope that I tied around my waist with shaking fingers, such was my relief that he'd found me. We set off, Secundus leading me as a man leads a dog, but I did not mind for I would rather be a found dog than a lost soul. Several people looked at the boy led by a rope, but thanks to the pack of Saint Peter not one called me hunchback or monster.

On we went, past men selling pies and men selling fish and women selling buns still warm. One man shouted that he had the greatest of relics, and held before him a board displaying bits of metal and cloth and glass. A fine lady pilgrim bent over the board, her handmaid beside her.

Secundus paused. He pointed to a sliver of wood. "And what would that be?"

The relic dealer pointed. "That is from the boat that carried Saint James all the way from the Holy Land to Spain."

How I marveled. Wood touched by the hand of Saint James—and anyone could buy it!

"I have just purchased his one other piece," announced the fine lady—and fine she was, for though she herself wore pilgrim wool, her handmaid's gown was trimmed in squirrel.

"Would you like to see?" She smiled at me—a true smile that felt like sunshine—and held out a slim gold case with as many compartments as I have fingers. Within each compartment lay a wee fragment of bone, except for one with a sliver of wood.

"Now I have nine saints plus the boat of Saint James." The lady turned to the relic dealer, and her smile hardened to iron. "What else have you to sell me?"

Dazzled by the fine lady's relics and smile, I followed Secundus. We came to a street where every booth and every door displayed crutches, men shouting that a crutch purchased in Saint-Peter's-Step would aid any cripple. Beyond was a street of cobblers, with more shoes and boots than I could imagine—shoes of leather and cloth, some with bells and some with laces, ladies' pattens with high soles so as not to tread in mud, and slippers for indoors, and thick boots that would last a man some years.

We came to a great square full of people: friars with cowls and nuns in their habits (though no nuns smuggling roosters!), and pilgrims with badges pinned to their hats. Men sold beeswax candles and beeswax feet, for wax is as precious as coins, and can be molded into any sort of offering. We reached the steps of a great church. Clouds of incense drifted out its doors whilst clouds of pilgrims drifted in. A preacher stood on the steps. "Let me tell you of Rome," he cried.

Secundus's head came up, and he pushed closer.

"The pope has declared this year—this year of our Lord 1350—as a Holy Year," continued the preacher. "All sinners who travel to Rome this year will receive a pardon."

For a moment Secundus's face held an expression of longing such as I never have seen.

"And the miracles to be found in Rome! Why, a woman leper touched the tomb of Saint Peter and was cured straightaway—"

"Lepers," Secundus scoffed. "That's all they ever speak of." He shouldered his way inside, and I had no choice but to follow.

This church, too, looked like the heart of a jewel. Color filled the windows, even in the gray dusk. The ceiling blazed with candles, and cloths hung on the walls. At the far end stood the altar, glittering with gold and candlelight. There sat a chest with open doors so that all might see its contents.

We made our way forward, and all about lay the injured and crippled, their feet painful to behold. Many had crutches. Men and women prayed before the chest, and eight guards stood around it with pikes, watching every pilgrim who approached.

Secundus studied the guards, and the windows behind them—tall narrow windows, topped with pointed arches—and the space around the altar. Closer we drew. I could see the precious relic. . . .

'Twas a shoe. A cracked man's shoe, dusty. The sort of shoe a poor man might give to a beggar.

Do you know who appeared at that moment? The crabby old man from the road. He shouted at the crowd as his son bore him forward, and waved a crutch at the guards. "I should like to kiss Saint Peter's shoe!"

"No one may touch this holy relic," answered a guard.

The old man flourished a glittering blue stone.

The guards looked at each other, and stepped aside so that the son could carry his father forward. He laid his father before the altar, and the old man placed his gem upon it. He smiled in triumph—

And he snatched up the shoe with his grubby old hand!

The crowd gasped.

"No!" cried the guards, lunging.

"No!" Secundus's eyes went wide.

The old man pressed the shoe to his lips, and set it down with a cry: "I am cured. 'Tis a miracle!" He pulled himself to his feet. Though he could not put weight on his crippled foot, he could walk well enough whilst crutching, and he crutched his way out of the church.

The pilgrims rejoiced at this miracle, and many knelt in prayer. But the guards scowled, and Secundus scowled as he watched the guards close ranks in front of the chest.

"Milord," I whispered, "the shoe almost was stolen."

"The guards did their job." But he did not sound happy, and he frowned as he pushed his way back to the street. "The crowds are worse than I feared. Let us find an inn—"

His head snapped up and his eyes grew hard.

I sniffed: bread and saffron and sweet wine and stewing apples, and a stink . . .

A dog in a doorway. A stinky old dog that broke wind in his sleep, loud enough for folk to hear, and to chuckle at the stench.

Secundus forced a smile. "Quite amusing," he said, though he did not sound amused.

How curious that he should not like stinky dogs when he

himself had a smell. I pondered this as I trailed him. Though Secundus's smell was somewhat different. If only I could name it . . .

At last we came upon a house where a plump wife sold eels and wine and beds by a fire. "What a sweet angel," she exclaimed when she saw me, for she did not notice my hump, and she ordered her daughter to serve us.

The daughter was young and slight but full of life, and she, too, did not notice my hump. She brought me a fine piece of honeycomb, and laughed like a burbling stream as the dogs pressed around my legs. "Why, you're as sweet as honey to them. I wish they loved me so." She asked where I came from, and sighed when I said I'd walked all the way from the manor. "How fine your home must be."

I looked around at the wide fireplace and the windows of waxed cloth. "'Tis not so fine as this." My goat shed had no windows at all.

She laughed her burbling laugh. "Listen to you! If you don't eat that honeycomb, I shall gobble it down myself." Off she trotted, leaving me to slip the honeycomb to the dogs (for in truth I do not care much for honey) and to marvel at how lovely it was to talk to another soul—a soul my own age who was even a girl!—without being jeered at or mocked. She treated me like I was a normal boy, just like the others.

So I settled myself in a corner, enjoying her laughter burbling over the hubbub, and I warned the dogs not to break wind or 'twould upset Secundus who was drinking with the other pilgrims, and they promised not to. A brindled mongrel bitch settled beside me with her four fat puppies, and she rested her head in my lap whilst they nursed and smiled her good dog smile, and another dog with shaggy black fur made certain that not a drop of honey remained on my fingers or behind my ears, and all the dogs lay close and the puppies, too, when they finished their meal, not one of them stinking, and at that moment I was as happy as ever I have been because I had dogs to love me and a miracle freshly witnessed, and not one person that day called me names, most especially not the daughter with her burbling laugh.

How fine it felt to walk without stares and curses. Without fearing stones. To enjoy the smiles of ladies, and the laughter of girls.

A notion sprouted like a weed inside my head: how fine

'twould be if my hump were gone, so that I could know more smiles and comfort and safety. If I could live as something other than hunchback or monster.

Stop, I ordered myself. *You should not think so, Boy. 'Tis not right.*

But the weed would not stop growing, no matter how I tried to pluck it.

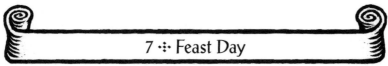

7 ·:· Feast Day

I awoke in a pile of dogs. Today was the feast day. Today Secundus and I would save the relic of Saint-Peter's-Step!

Around me snored other pilgrims. Secundus himself had claimed the table, and he lay like a corpse with his hat over his face, clutching his staff to his chest.

The plump wife bustled about as her daughter stirred a pot on the fire. The girl giggled at the sight of me in a pile of dogs, and her giggle lightened the room.

Beside the fire sat a blind man telling a story—a story the daughter had heard, for she nodded, but pilgrims gathered around the man as they woke, and I gathered, too, for who does not like a good story? The tale began in the Holy Land, where Saint Peter set out to spread the Good Word. He crossed the salty sea—so the blind man recounted—and landed on the shores of France, and walked all the way to a mountain. There he met a beggar woman so poor that she had no shoes even in the snowy depths of winter. So Saint Peter gave his shoes to the beggar woman and returned to Rome, where he later was killed by the wicked Roman emperor. The beggar woman sold one shoe for food, but she kept the other because it was holy, and pilgrims came to see the shoe of Saint Peter, and in time the monastery of Saint-Peter's-Mount flourished atop the mountain.

(Here the blind man paused. The daughter filled a bowl with stew and wrapped his hands around the bowl, and he thanked her as he ate with his fingers.)

A town grew at the base of the mountain, the town of Saint-Peter's-Step. But the pilgrims who climbed Saint-Peter's-Mount rarely lingered in the town below, and the monks of the monastery gave no thought to the needs of their neighbors. Then came the pestilence. The cowardly monks in the monastery left the relic unprotected, and the earnest townsfolk brought the shoe down to safety. Now great wealth came to Saint-Peter's-Step, each day bringing more people, all from the blessings of Saint Peter's shoe.

The daughter nodded, listening, and smiled though the blind man could not see.

"And the miracles," the blind man sighed. "Only yesterday an old man crawled twelve leagues to get here. He crawled to the altar and kissed Saint Peter's shoe, and at once his crippled foot was healed and he danced his way out of the church!"

I gasped in delight. I had witnessed this miracle! To be fair, the old man had not crawled or danced, but 'twas his mind as much as his foot that had been healed, which is a miracle indeed for one so crabby—

A poke in the back gave me a start: Secundus. "Come, Boy."

So I gathered my stick and I patted the dogs and I waved good-bye to the daughter who burbled with laughter. She said the dogs would miss me, which made me hope that she would miss me, too, and I followed Secundus out into the morn.

Today's crowds were even thicker. Secundus checked the safety of the pack on my back because a crowd such as this has busy fingers, and he tested the rope around my waist. "How do you feel? Can you climb?"

"Oh, yes, milord." I tugged the rope to show him how fine I was.

"Prepare yourself. Events will occur quickly. You must move fast, and do what I say."

I nodded, my pulse quickening. We had a relic to save.

We made our way to the church steps where the same preacher promised the miracles to be found in Rome. Secundus handed me the silver cup that Cook had given me one two three days past, though verily it felt like one two three years. "Wave it high, Boy," he said as we entered. "We have an offering!" he shouted. "Make way that this boy may gift the church of Saint-Peter's-Step."

The crowd oohed at the silver, and let us pass.

Saint Peter's shoe rested in its chest with guards all around. Before the shoe knelt rich and poor and young and old, men and women both.

Secundus released his hold on the rope and nodded me toward the altar steps. The high windows behind the altar stood open, airing out the smell of incense and pilgrims.

I knelt, resting my stick beside me. I lay the cup upon the coins and tokens and candles and wax, remembering the night Sir Jacques toasted the birth of his son. I prayed for milady and her three babies. I prayed that Sir Jacques might be cured of his terrible injury. As I'd promised, I prayed for Cook: "Please, Saint Peter, preserve Cook from eternal damnation."

I glanced at Secundus. He stood studying the guards.

"And please, Saint Peter," I whispered. "Please, I am only a goatherd, and—a monster. . . . But please, Saint Peter, cure my hump so no one stares."

There. I had said the words aloud.

"Amen." I waited.

Perhaps Saint Peter would answer my prayer later.

I climbed to my feet, rope in hand. Secundus stood, not moving.

The crowd pressed forward. Near us a young mother held a pink-cheeked baby chewing two fingers. The mother looked in fright at the mass of pilgrims. Even with the open windows, the air hung thick with incense and candle smoke, and no breeze moved the cloths hanging on the walls.

A woman screamed that she was suffocating. Another woman screamed, and a man. The pink-cheeked baby began to cry.

"Milord . . ."

"Be patient," Secundus murmured. "They will come when the third hour rings."

The bells began to toll in the tower above us—bells marking the third hour of prayers.

A great clamoring rose behind us, at the entrance to the church.

"Thieves!" someone cried.

"The monks!" cried another. "They've sent fighters!"

The monks. Secundus was right!

"We've come for our relic," a man bellowed. Metal clashed, and the crowd pressed away from the battle—pressed us so that I feared we'd be trampled. The mother screamed, clutching her baby.

The altar guards stiffened, their pikes pointing outward. Secundus watched, frowning. "Go aid your brethren," he shouted.

"Milord, the baby—"

"Move, men!" Secundus commanded. But the guards did not.

"Milord, the baby will be crushed—" We must protect the relic, I knew, but a baby is more important than a shoe.

"Forget the—" He spun to me, his face lighting up. "You are right! Climb, Boy. Climb to the window. I will toss the baby to you."

'Twas a madcap solution, but better than naught. Better than letting a baby get crushed.

The guards gripped their pikes, and did their best to peer over the crowd, trying to catch sight of the battle. They did not notice me wiggling like a salamander betwixt their legs toward the wall. Up I climbed, gripping rocks and tapestries, the rope trailing behind me. I reached the windowsill.

"Ho, Boy!" bellowed Secundus. He snatched up the baby.

"No!" shrieked the pretty young mother, lunging for her child. The pilgrims around her screamed.

"Boy!" yelled Secundus, so loudly that the guards turned to look, and the mother, and the pilgrims. He cocked his arms—

I struggled to balance on the narrow windowsill. What was he doing? No good person would ever throw a child—

Secundus tossed me the baby.

Till the end of my days I shall remember that moment. The crowd stood in shock, the mouth of every man and every woman hanging open in the shape of an egg, as the baby flew up, up to me. The guards turned, their eyes wide, watching. The baby's mouth, too, was egg shaped, and its arms flailed in the smoky air.

I must save this baby or it will die.

I reached out, my legs gripping the sill, every eye in the church upon me.

The baby soared—the crowd gasped—

I grabbed the baby with both my hands, and pulled us to safety.

The baby stared at me for a long second—and released a wail of outrage.

"My baby!" cried the mother, hurling herself past the guards. She grabbed the rope around my waist and climbed. Never would I have thought a mother so nimble, but right soon she was perched beside me, clasping her baby.

At once the crowd's screaming redoubled, and the crash of weapons, and battle.

"Boy!" shouted Secundus, near tugging me off the window as he, too, climbed my rope. He hauled himself up with a triumphant laugh, pulling the rope behind him. "Jump," he cried, and I jumped onto the roof below the window, away from the panic and fighting, and I helped the mother creep down the mossy tiles, and I held the baby as she jumped down to the street, and lowered the wailing baby to her.

"May God bless you," cried the pretty young mother. "May God bless you forever and ever."

"Be off with you," Secundus snapped, landing beside us. "Come, Boy." He dashed down an alley that stank of cats. I trotted behind, thrumming with excitement as shouts echoed from the church. I'd saved a baby's life! A baby and a mother. And possibly—although this did not matter so much—possibly even my own.

The alley emptied onto a street, and another, and a thick gate with two guards, and we were outside the walls of the town.

"We did it." Secundus beamed in delight. The badges on his hat twinkled in the sun.

"We saved them!"

"What? Ah. Yes. We saved the—" He sniffed.

But all I smelled was rotting turnips. "Don't worry, milord. Turnips smell like dog wind."

"What?"

"The dog last night—you did not like the smell. Turnips and dog wind smell the same."

He barked a laugh. "Ah, that mongrel breaking wind. You

are right: 'tis the smell of bad turnips. Ah, Boy, I will miss you."

Miss me?

"You surely can climb," he chuckled. "And you're a clever one to think of that baby."

I could not help but smile, for pride is the downfall of every soul.

We walked, Secundus with his thoughts and I with mine, the rope trailing behind me. I had witnessed two miracles, I had: the old man healed and the baby in flight. I had walked across water and seen the very shoe of Saint Peter. (Whatever became of the shoe, I wondered . . . but a baby matters more than a shoe.) I'd talked with a girl who did not call me a monster, and I'd received a smile from a fine lady. And I'd prayed for Cook as she ordered. How fine it would be to report this. Perhaps Cook would no longer shout at me so.

Glad I was that we had three days to return to the manor, for I would need every minute to set these stories to memory. Perhaps one day when I was old and blind, I would tell these tales for a small bit of honey I could give to the dogs. Perhaps I'd have more than dogs to talk to, and goats. Perhaps I'd have a friend whose laughter burbled like water on rocks. . . .

We arrived at a spot where the road approached the river-bank. Upstream I could see a fording place with a long wet rope and a herdsman leading oxen through the knee-deep water, his hands gripping the cable.

Secundus studied his book. He pointed. "You'll need to cross there."

"Yes, milord . . ." I did not care for the way he said *you* as though it would be me alone.

He frowned, and at once my heart stopped, for though I cannot read words I have skill at reading people, and I remembered how he said he would miss me, and in that instant I realized he'd just sent me away.

8 ⋅⁝⋅ A Fork in the Road

"Please, milord!" I dropped to my knees. "Please do not dismiss me."

"Stand up. I needed a boy who could climb through a window. I do not need that anymore."

"Please, milord—"

"Silence! Give me the pack. Where is the stick?"

The stick! "I'm sorry, I lost it—"

"You lost it? How am I to carry the rib?"

"I can find you another—" I dashed down the path, but such is the world that a stick was not to be found. Behind me, Secundus clutched his book, seething. His silence gave me time to think. I would never find the manor, I knew: it lay somewhere west, and west is a very broad distance. And even if

I did know the route, I could not walk alone. Good men would think me a runaway or worse. I'd be murdered by brigands, or eaten by wolves.

But another thought crept into my head as a vine creeps betwixt stones, and this thought featured vanity. Not once since Secundus tied his pack to my hump had I been called hunchback or monster. I enjoyed that, I did. I enjoyed getting smiles. I should like to enjoy them some more.

With every step this thought grew inside me. The goats would not miss me—they'd miss my company, I should like to think, but they did not need me, for goats are clever and tough. Ox had other victims. As for Cook, I had donated the cup and prayed for her soul, and could report so. But I did not need to report it quite yet.

I patted the pack on my back. My heart lifted at its soft warmth.

"What are you doing?" Secundus snapped.

"Begging your pardon, milord, I am making sure the relic is safe." *Appreciating its protection. Wishing I could wear it longer.* "Milord?" I asked. So carefully.

"What?"

"I do so enjoy—I know 'tis not my place—but I like bearing your burden—"

"My *burden*?"

"Your—your pack, milord—"

Secundus spun so quick that I feared I'd be slapped. "You have no notion of my burden. No notion at all." He brandished his book: "Look."

Pages of words. Words, and drawings, and lines I did not understand. Whole pages crossed out, or written to the very edges. "This is my quest. Decades—centuries!—of knowledge. The seven relics of Saint Peter. I have maps, I have floor plans, I have . . . secrets. I learned only six months ago of the monks' plan to attack. Just before—before Paris. That was the last detail. Or so I thought." Without warning he swung at me.

I flinched—but he was not striking me, no; he was clawing at the pack on my shoulders. He was *almost* clawing, for no sooner did he touch the pack than he screamed.

"*That* is my burden," he spat. Off he strode.

I followed, rope trailing. What else could I do?

"Gather six relics and take them to Saint Peter's tomb in Rome. Rib tooth thumb shin dust skull tomb. Simple. What could I have missed, in all my research? One fact, barely worth mentioning: I cannot touch the saint's bones!" He glared at the scar on his palm.

"Rome, milord? Did you say Rome?" Secundus was headed to Rome?

With a snap, he broke a branch from a tree.

Rome! Why, Rome is the city of miracles—everyone knows this. Men are healed both body and soul when they reach the tomb of Saint Peter. "Milord?"

"Give me my pack." He held out the branch.

"Please let me serve you."

"What?" His eyes narrowed. "Why?"

"Because . . . I should like to carry this pack. So you are not burned." *Because I should like to reach the tomb of Saint Peter, so that he can make me a regular boy.*

I gathered the rope that trailed behind me, though mud soiled my hands. That is how diligent a servant I was: I would cover myself in muck for Secundus. "You could be my master, and I'd be your boy. I'd serve you as I served Sir Jacques. . . ." Carefully I untied the knot.

Secundus strode down the path.

I raced after him, and handed him the rope.

He tossed it aside and strode on.

I kept pace. "I can hurry. I can walk as fast as a man." One two three days prior I had been so frightened of this pilgrim that I would have done anything to avoid him, and now I wanted naught so much as to serve him. *I must get to Rome. There, at the tomb, Saint Peter will grant me a miracle.* Then Cook would accept me, and Ox, and no one would sneer or throw stones, and I would no longer be a monster.

We came to a fork in the road. To the left flowed the river with its wide shallow ford. To the right rose a path.

Secundus stopped.

I halted, panting. I had kept pace.

I stood with the pack warm on my hump, and I bowed my head as a good servant should. Dearly did I want to kneel, but I sensed this would not sway him; indeed, the reverse.

"You eat naught." He did not look at me.

"No, milord." There was more I could have said, but didn't.

"You can carry . . ." His mouth twisted. "You'll carry my relics till you delay me. Then—"

"Yes, milord." I would never delay him. Not once.

He studied me, from my old red hood to my tattered too-big boots. "Come." He swept up the path. Away from the river. Away from the manor. Toward Rome.

Oh, my heart leaped in my chest, but I spoke not a whisper. I kept inside me many words I might have said. I did not say *Thank you, master.* I did not say *I must go to Rome to lose my hump.* I did not say *I shall tell you the truth, master: I am a monster, not a boy.*

And so I was a liar. A lying monster en route to Rome. Wicked me.

II

The Relic Thief

9 ⋅⋮⋅ Tooth, the Second

Up we climbed, up and up, but however I panted I did not slow, for I was going to Rome!

I go to Rome to become a boy.

How good these words sounded.

The hill grew steeper till the path sprouted steps and became a staircase—a staircase slippery and old, missing stones. Several times I fell, banging my shins, but I did not tarry.

Secundus paused, cheeks flushed, and pulled out his book. "Does that rock look like a resting cow?"

Indeed it did, now that I noticed. And the drawing in his book looked just like the rock.

"That's the trail we'll need later." He studied other drawings, and words around the drawings, and words crossed out.

"The monastery of Saint-Peter's-Mount. . . Many places to hide a tooth." He looked up, and his frown changed to a grin. "And so we will have to barter." He reached into his purse for a dusty object, and just as quick returned it.

I gasped: "The shoe!" Saint Peter's shoe, from the altar at Saint-Peter's-Step!

Again he grinned: "Come, Boy." Off he set.

"But—" That moment when Secundus tossed me the baby— every pilgrim had turned to watch me. Every woman. Every man. Every guard . . . Every face, I realized, except Secundus. For in that moment he was snaking his hand to the altar. "But milord, you said we must *protect* the shoe."

"Do you think it'd be safe in that mob? And the baby—if not for us, the baby would have been trampled. The baby *and* the shoe. A brilliant diversion, Boy. Brilliant."

"But don't the townsfolk want their relic?"

"You heard the blind man—they took it from the monastery. We are returning it."

But you risked a baby's life, I wanted to say. *You risked mine. You say words that sound true but confuse me. You said—* "Milord, you said that relics burn you."

"Clever child. So how can I carry this shoe? Because of course it is fake . . . Ah. Here we are at last."

The staircase ended at a crumbling wall sprouting ivy, its gate sagging: the monastery of Saint-Peter's-Mount. A fortress it was, though in decline. No sound met my ears save the whistle of wind. No one in this place ever laughed like the burble of water.

Secundus squared his shoulders and entered.

I followed, stunned yet at his revelation. Secundus had the shoe!

Grass squirmed between paving stones. Weeds choked mounds of dirt topped with crosses: pestilence had struck this place hard.

A bent gatekeeper shuffled toward us. A word and a coin from Secundus, and he led us into a great room that blocked the wind but stored the chill. There sat a man, his head bent in prayer.

He is praying for his men, I realized. Small wonder he looked worried.

"Greetings, Brother Abbot. I apologize for our interruption." Secundus laid a thin gold coin on the table. "Might I have a moment of your time?"

The abbot gazed at the coin, and at Secundus. His eyes traveled over the badges on Secundus's hat. "Please. I can't offer wine, I'm afraid. . . ."

"Wine is for pleasant afternoons. I am here on business. You are, I believe, in need of a relic."

A relic my master carries, thought I, though I tried to keep this thought from my face. *A relic that men now fight for in the town below.*

The abbot slapped the table. "The townsfolk say they *rescued* it, but no, they stole it as we tended our dying brothers. If we yet had the shoe, pilgrims would come. . . ."

"Ah." Secundus smiled his smile. "That happens to be why I am here. Some time ago—many years—I heard a most extraordinary story about a monk. A monk who served in the Mother of All the Churches in Rome, wherein rests the head of Saint Peter."

The abbot's expression slid toward unease.

"Ah. I believe you know of what I speak. For this monk—so the story went—had no decency within him. One night whilst guarding the altar, he decided to see the relic for himself. He looked upon it . . . and he stole a tooth."

The abbot watched Secundus with hard eyes.

"A tooth from the head of Saint Peter. This scoundrel, as you seem to know, fled Rome, and at length arrived in France, at a monastery atop a mountain. A monastery dedicated to Saint Peter, which, the scoundrel believed, would in some way ease his sin. The monastery accepted the relic—the tooth—and the man then leading the monastery promised to return it to Rome."

"Cannot possibly . . . No one knows. . . ."

"But that abbot never did."

"This happened—if this happened—long ago. They are all of them dead."

"Ah. Death." Secundus smiled. "You and I know that such a relic is worth gold enough to pave this mountain. But if you were to announce its existence, the pope would deny it, for Saint Peter belongs only in the pope's holy city. If a humble monastery were to claim a piece of the first pope—to imply that pilgrims need not trek to Rome . . . Imagine the response of the churchmen. Of the innkeepers. You might be put before the Inquisition. Theft, falsehood . . ."

"Not theft! I mean—'twas not stolen. The tooth leaped into the poor monk's hand."

"Ah. That is a better version. I am not sure who would believe it."

"Saint Peter wanted us to have it."

"That may well be. But it is of faint benefit to you now. You have in your possession a treasure you cannot in any way use." Secundus reached into his purse. "I am asking to exchange it for a treasure you can." He set Saint Peter's shoe on the table.

The abbot gasped. He gaped at the shoe, and at Secundus, and even at me, a hundred thoughts on his face. . . . He set his jaw, picked up the coin, and swept from the room.

We waited, my master and I. Secundus wiped his forehead. His cheeks glowed, and his eyes. "Do you know how to fight, Boy?"

"No, milord. . . . I can run, though," I added, for pride's sake.

"Prepare to run. The abbot will either bring what I want, or he will claim this shoe by force. . . . They have sold the tapestries, it seems."

Now I noticed the hooks in the stonework, and the emptiness of the walls. This room would be lovely hung with tapestries, and candles burning, and a fire.

Footsteps. The abbot returned. Alone.

Secundus's shoulders relaxed.

The abbot set a box on the table—a wee gold box bearing the image of a curly-bearded man with a key: Saint Peter.

"Open it," Secundus murmured.

The abbot scowled but complied. Inside lay a yellow tooth, a tooth worn and old and quite unappealing.

"Take it, Boy," said Secundus. "Leave the box."

I picked up the tooth. It felt warm . . . though anything would feel warm in that cold room.

With a glance at Secundus, the abbot snatched up the shoe—the dusty cracked shoe that was named for Saint Peter—and clutched it.

Secundus stood. "An excellent trade. May the shoe bring you all the blessings you deserve." He headed for the door. I trotted behind as a servant ought, and though my neck prickled, I did not look back.

We exited, the gatekeeper nowhere in sight.

We are safe, thought I—

A great noise, more deafening than thunder, assaulted us. I screamed.

"Those are bells, Boy." Secundus laughed. "Have you never heard church bells?"

Of course I knew church bells. But I had never heard them so close.

"A wonderful sound, is it not?" he shouted over the racket.

It is loud is what it is, I wanted to say.

"He is announcing a miracle!"

The din shook the ground, the distant hilltops hurling back echoes.

We hurried down the rough stone staircase. In the silence between the bells, I could hear voices—men climbing toward us, singing. The monks!

We reached the rock that was shaped like a resting cow, and ducked behind it. Not a moment too soon, for a company of monks appeared on the stairs. Other men walked with them— fighters, they looked like, with swords and bloodied staffs, and bloodied bandages, too; the monks bore the injured. Monks cannot fight, and so must use others to wage their battles. But even the fighters sang as they trudged up the steps.

I held my breath, praying to the rib on my back and the tooth in my hand that Secundus and I wouldn't be found—not by monks, nor by fighters! Beside me, Secundus put his fist to his lips.

One by one the men passed us, singing. Not one looked behind the cow-shaped rock. . . .

They were gone.

I exhaled in relief.

Secundus exhaled, and straightened. "Hurry," he whispered, setting off along a trail. A trail away from monks. Away from the town. Quickly we walked, and never did I relax my grip on the treasure in my fist.

He stopped, finally. "Show me."

I opened my hand: a relic old and yellow but most clearly toothlike.

He handed me a scrap of silk the color of the sun. "Store it in the pack. Carefully."

I wrapped the relic in the glorious color, and by twisting and straining opened the pack's mouth. Secundus watched, not helping. At last I slipped in the tooth.

"Good." He wiped his forehead and walked on.

"'Tis good your monk friend did not see us," I added. How fine it felt to be clever.

He frowned. "Who?"

"The monk who told you about the attack on the church.

Six months ago . . ." Did he not remember?

Secundus barked a laugh. "Ah. Him. That monk died of old age. Now hurry."

Onward we walked. Mist settled around us, and drizzle. My goatskin grew heavy with wet. At last we came to a road, and a cottage—a cottage lately used by sheep, but I did not care. Secundus kicked away the mess and spread his cloak on the floor. "Here, Boy."

"Thank you, milord, but I do not need—"

"Lie down," he ordered. "You need to rest."

I collapsed on the cloak, for everyone prefers wool to cold dirt. Oh, was I tired.

Secundus secured the door and settled himself in a corner. He lit a small candle retrieved from one of his pockets, and studied his book with bright eyes. From another pocket he pulled out a quill, and a wee bottle plugged with a cork.

I watched with wide eyes. "Milord—you can write, too?"

"Remarkable: I can read and write both." He dipped the quill into the bottle of ink, and with a smile crossed out a word. He flourished the book so I could see writing that looked like this:

~~Tooth.~~

"So now I have the tooth and the rib. My informants have served me well."

"Informants?"

"People who give me information. Every soul has information. Like that monk. My task is to gather the bits." He blew on the ink. "Now I need only thumb shin dust skull tomb."

"Thumb shin dust skull home," I repeated.

"No, Boy—*tomb*, not *home*. A tomb that gets me to paradise."

10 ⁘ A Bath

Thunder—a soft rumbling . . .

I awoke to a tomcat on my chest. He was orange and striped, both ears ragged, and he sat like a warlord at rest. *Mmm,* said he. *You make a marvelous bed.*

"I wonder"—Secundus's voice reached me from across the cottage—"if we should wager on which animal I will find on you each morn. . . . Now my cloak is covered in hair."

The tomcat yawned, not sorry at all. His ears pricked. He stiffened, and bolted through a hole in the wall.

Now I could hear: jingling. A hubbub of rough male song.

"Quick, Boy!" Secundus grabbed his staff and dashed outside. Like a rabbit I followed him into the hedge.

Around a bend came a company of knights, and squires with

84

banners, and stout men leading an oxcart. Oh, they looked glorious, their armor glittering. Well could I remember Sir Jacques adorned thus, prepared for a day full of sport.

But Secundus bit his lip. "Do not see us," he whispered. "I cannot die. Not now . . ." He gripped his staff so hard that his knuckles were white.

The knights sang, and one knight beat a tune on the hilt of his sword. Sir Jacques had a sword like that, so heavy I could not lift it. . . . They passed a jug betwixt them, drinking deeply. Where had they acquired such a homey item?

I glanced at Secundus, who seemed to be holding his breath. My heart pounded inside me. If he was feared, then I should fear doubly.

A knight brandishing a torch bellowed that the jug was empty. A squire rushed to fill it from a wine cask on the oxcart. The cart held a mattress, and a carved chest, and a hoof . . . no, a goat. Two goats. Two dead goats.

I tried my best not to scream.

The knight with the torch paused at the cottage that Secundus and I had just fled. His fellows laughed and clapped as he tossed the torch inside.

No one bothered to check if the cottage was empty.

I twitched in horror. But the wicked knights applauded.

Flames clawed through the thatch, the smoke puking upward, as the knights called for even more wine.

A knight's horse—a chestnut stallion with a scarred nose—turned toward the hedge. His ears pricked forward. *Ha . . . I smell creatures.*

My heart stopped. *No, good charger,* I whispered. *Pay us no notice. Please.*

The knight frowned, following his horse's gaze. Flames leaped, snapping.

Beside me, Secundus sucked his teeth.

The charger's nostrils flared, and he huffed the sound that a fierce creature makes when it hungers to lunge. *Ha! I will fight you.*

Please, fine stallion, I begged. *We mean you no harm. You will have battles soon enough, and grain, and beer*—for his rider seemed one who would feast his horse whilst starving his bride.

Peering into the hedge, the rider drew his sword.

The roof collapsed in a flurry of sparks.

Grain, horse! Beer. But please look elsewhere. . . .

The great charger met my gaze through the leaves of the hedge . . . and shook his head with a jangle of tack, his lips blowing a noise more expressive than speech. He turned away. *Ha. I've better creatures to fight.*

Scowling, the rider, too, turned away, sheathing his weapon.

With a toss of his handsome cruel head, the charger trotted off. The other knights followed, their squires behind them. Away rolled the cart of riches and death.

The walls of the cottage fell with a crash.

Secundus wiped his forehead. "In my day such barbarians would be strung up like flags."

I worked air into my chest. "Are they brigands?"

"Worse."

What could be worse than brigands? Brigands are wicked outlaws who ambush honest travelers, and rob them, and sometimes even take their lives. "Are they . . . wolves?"

He snorted. "Almost. They're English. Soldiers . . . they used to be soldiers. The English king sent them to France to make war, but he no longer pays them and will not bring them home." He eased his way out of the hedge to the road churned to mud.

I shuddered to think of our fate if we'd yet been in the

cottage. *Please, Saint Peter, keep me safe from the English. And please protect the manor....*

Secundus brushed leaves from his robe. His robe—

"Milord, your cloak!" I turned to the burning ruin. On the floor, his cloak had been . . .

He set out walking. "Do not worry yourself. 'Tis ash now. Perhaps it's gone to hell." He snorted.

"Milord?" I did not care for talk of hell.

"'Tis an old joke of mine; don't worry yourself. The cloak will be awaiting those soldiers when they arrive.... Ah, a crossroad." He pulled out his book, tapping the pages as he read.

The sun climbed and the day warmed, and with time my terror faded. Often we looked back, and cocked our heads to listen, but the English knights were elsewhere. "Barbarians," Secundus muttered. I prayed for the souls the English would meet.

We came to a crossroads marked with a finely carved cross, and as usual Secundus consulted his book. He flipped forward. . . . He stared at me. "I have a boy with me now. A boy who can climb. Who can serve . . . You can serve, yes?"

"Oh, yes. I poured Sir Jacques's wine, and brought washbasins, and carried his platters—"

"How long have you worn those clothes?"

"Since they were given to me." *Never reveal yourself,* and never I had. The tunic had not left my body for a year at least.

"You smell like a goat." He sniffed his armpit and made a face. "We both need a bath."

All the day we walked. We passed barley fields two years gone, fierce young trees sprouting between the dead stalks, turning the field back into forest. We passed empty villages, their residents moved to town or paradise—villages empty, but at least not burned by the English.

We came to a town, a busy town with only some of its houses vacant. Secundus found an inn with a fire, and left me there, and at once I fell asleep in a pile of dogs.

I awoke sometime later to his gentle prod: "Boy, I've something for you."

Oh, did he look different. His face was polished and shiny, and his robe was brushed clean, and he smelled not of sweat nor sourness, but lavender.

He led me to a room with a tub of gray water. "That is a bath. You will get in it."

"But I'll get wet."

He smiled. "That's the point. You will remove my pack and your clothes and scrub yourself with soap." He pointed to a whitish lump. "Most particularly your hair. Then dress your-self"—he nodded to a fresh pile of clothes—"leaving off your goatskin. Do you understand?"

"Yes, milord." Soap in one's hair: whosoever heard of that?

He left, whistling. Fancy my master cheerful.

I glared at the bath. Yes, I had seen folk washing. But not me. *Never reveal yourself.* I never took my clothes off at all.

But I must obey. I blocked the door with a trunk so no one could enter, and untied the pack with a prayer, and removed my goatskin so stinky but warm, and tugged off my boots and my hose. Shyly I peeled off my tunic. But I left on my hood.

With great caution I tested the water. Hot it must have been for Secundus, but warm enough for me. I eased in, watching the gray water darken . . . perhaps I was a bit grimy. I leaned back, marveling because I had never before sat in water so deep, and then set to work scrubbing. Fingers, toes, between my toes, armpits and elbows and knees . . . I even scraped under my nails with a stick. At last with great reluc-tance I removed my hood and poured water over my head as milady did with Sir Jacques, and I did not drown but almost.

I scrubbed with soap as my master bade, and scrubbed again because the first soap did not lather, and scrubbed my ears and my neck, but I did not soap my hump because that I must never touch. Making quite sure no one could see, I climbed out of the tub like a dog, and dried myself whilst the room filled with the smell of chickens. Quick I turned to the clothes.

Oh, the tunic! 'Twas blue, well-worn so as to be tremendously soft, and big enough to cover my hump and to allow me to grow. The pack felt quite fine atop the blue cloth. "Can you see, Saint Peter?" I asked. "Can you see how grand we look?" The hose were the brown of a nut, equally worn and soft.

Footsteps. "Are you clean?" Secundus called.

"Yes, milord. Thank you, milord, for these clothes—"

"What have you done to the door?"

I dashed to move the trunk.

"Let us see you. . . . Is your hair always like that?"

I blushed, Ox's taunts in my ears, and reached for the hood. *Princess,* he had called me.

"No, leave it. It's fine." Secundus smiled, his eyes bright, his cheeks rosy.

At dinner he asked many questions of the other diners, and was quick to buy them wine, and he wrote down their words in his book. The men grinned at my curls but did not call me princess or monster, for which I was grateful. A girl with long braids refilled their cups, and she shot me a look as I sat with the dogs. I scowled, and scowled more when she reached for my hair. "Please don't touch it," I asked—

But 'twas my sleeve she wanted, not my curls. "This was my brother's," she whispered. "And the hose. Before he passed."

Oh. "I'm so sorry"—'twas the least I could say. I repeated words I'd learned from Father Petrus. "We lose those we love. Such is the nature of life."

She nodded, her gaze far away. "But we don't lose their memories, do we? And his clothes have found a good home. . . . Wine for you? Some bread?"

I shook my head because bread I don't care for, and thanked her for her kindness, and I snuggled down with the dogs because dogs always love me and because they, too, might want to touch the tunic of a boy they had lost.

And then—I shall tell you where Secundus and I went after

dinner. To a bedroom! A bedroom with a bed, with pillows and mostly clean sheets.

I stared so hard that Secundus laughed. "Have you never seen a bed before?"

"Never to sleep in."

"Well, sleep now; you've earned it."

So I climbed in without undressing because *never reveal yourself.* Had the boy slept in this bed? I added him to my prayers, promising to care for his tunic and hose. So much had happened this day: the awful English knights, our walking, the bath, my new clothes. . . .

Secundus settled himself on the floor.

I sat up. How rude of me! "Milord, I will take the floor—the bed is for you—"

"No, Boy. I prefer the feel of the cold. Truly." He coughed, and stretched out. I pictured his eyes shining in the darkness. . . .

His bright eyes. His flushed cheeks. His cough.

I gasped. How had I not realized? Secundus was burning with fever.

My master was terribly ill.

11 ∴ The Story of the Tear-Soaked Veil

I dreamed that Ox was jeering at my curls, calling me a pretty girl, and I woke up gasping in the dark. With both hands I held my curls down, and repeated the words *I go to Rome to become a boy* over and over again till I could fall back asleep.

The next morning we set off, though Secundus made me leave behind my hood as well as my goatskin, for he claimed they both smelled. So I held down my curls as I walked, wishing the sun did not shine so bright on my hair.

He grinned: "Do not fret, Boy. They're an asset."

I did not know what *asset* meant, however, and feared it might be an insult. In the daylight I could see the fevered pink of his cheeks and the unhealthy shine of his eyes. But I did not mention it. I kept pace, and waited at crossroads whilst he studied his book, and ducked behind him when he asked directions, for I did not like others to see me.

Our road climbed and turned; the crest, when we reached it, revealed hills in every shade of green, and a sky of woolly clouds. A walled church with a fine spire stood on a distant peak; on another hill rose a castle that glowed in the sun.

Secundus smiled, and he shut his book with a snap. "My next . . . acquisition."

"The thumb"—'twas nice to think of something other than sickness and hair.

"Do you remember every blessed word I say? Yes, the thumb. But it will not be easy." He headed down the hill, speaking to me and to himself, telling a story.

The story, as it happened, involved both the distant walled church and the castle. The Castle of Gold, it is called, because the yellow stone glows so prettily. Many decades ago, a fine lady lived in the Castle of Gold, a lady with terrible sadness because she could not have a baby. She pilgrimed to Spain, to Canterbury, to Rome, but her prayers were not answered. At last she returned home and sought comfort at a nearby convent. She wept so hard during her prayers that her veil became soaked with tears. Within a year, she gave birth to a boy.

Word spread of this miraculous birth, and soon women from many towns journeyed to the convent to pray. Their prayers, too, were answered. The lady of the Castle of Gold gave the convent her tear-soaked veil and half her lands, and other grateful mothers gifted the convent so that it grew to be a great church. Every year the nuns washed the tear-soaked veil in wine, and sold the blessed wash-wine in small glass vials. Women from many lands now pilgrimed here, and men too.

A fine story this was, for who does not want to hear about babies—but 'twas only half the tale. The other half involved the son—the very son of the Castle of Gold. This fine lord, though he should be grateful indeed for his mother's prayers and efforts, resented that she had given so much land to the convent, land that he believed should be his. His sons and grandsons and great-grandsons believed as well. The present lord of the Castle of Gold at this very minute was in Paris suing to get the lands back.

The lord had left his wife behind, and this is where the story grew sad. Ten years they'd been married, and in ten years the wife had not had a child. She begged to pray to the tear-soaked veil, but the nuns would not allow her to visit. The nuns would not even allow her a vial of wash-wine—not till the lord ended his lawsuit.

"But that is so awful," I cried. "This poor wife has naught to do with her husband's meanness."

Secundus agreed. The wife herself came from a fine noble family. In fact, an ancestor had fought in the First Crusade, and had helped to capture Jerusalem. The pope in gratitude gave him a most holy relic: a sword that held in its hilt the thumb of Saint Peter. This ancestor used the sword in every battle he fought, gripping Saint Peter in his very fist, and thanks to Saint Peter he won. His descendants wielded the sword till the blade wore clear away. The hilt with its precious bone relic remained the family's most treasured possession, and served as the wife's dowry.

The spire of the convent was quite close now—I could see it between the budding oak trees. "You mean," I asked, "that this wife who cannot have children has the thumb of Saint Peter?" 'Twas like tracing a spiderweb, all these lines. "We should help her, don't you think?" A brilliant thought struck me. "We could bring her the veil!"

Secundus smiled. "That's a clever notion. If only I'd come up with it."

"She'd be so happy that she'd give us the thumb. But . . ." My joy dimmed. "Why would the nuns give us the veil?"

"Ah. An inn," Secundus exclaimed. "Let us refresh our-selves, for the night will be long." So I did not get an answer.

The inn was crowded with travelers gossiping like crows whilst they dined. Several asked if we had been threatened.

"Threatened by what?" asked Secundus, pouring wine.

Brigands, we learned, had attacked a group of pilgrims not twenty leagues distant. "It was terrible, terrible," a peddler reported.

"Terrible," echoed Secundus, carving himself a slice of roast.

A man leaned in—a messenger, judging from his fine clothes, and the locked pouch on his belt, and his general air of importance. A messenger to some fine nobleman. "They say the brigands were so wicked that they smelled of brimstone."

Secundus flinched. With fierce strokes he returned to his roast. "Hmph. What other news have you?"

I did not know this word *brimstone*. But I knew other scents Secundus was feared of—rotting turnips, and windy dogs . . .

I crept to the messenger who sat cracking nuts with the butt of his knife. "Excuse me," I whispered. "'Tis only—did the brigands smell of farts?"

Well. If I had dropped a snake into a henhouse, I could not have caused a greater disruption. The messenger roared with laughter, and repeated my question whilst holding my arm so I could not duck away. My face near burned off as every man wiped his eyes in mirth, repeating *did they smell of farts?* for a fine jest cannot simply be swallowed but must be burped up again and again.

But Secundus did not laugh. He stuffed the roast in his mouth and gulped down his wine. "Come, Boy," he ordered, his voice cutting through the laughter. "We've a quest to complete." We left the inn soon thereafter, and hurried along without speaking.

I worked up my courage. "Milord? What's brimstone?"

"'Tis the stench of hell," he answered, not breaking stride.

That made sense, for neither farts nor turnips smell of heaven. But—oh! "Did those brigands come from hell?"

He snorted a laugh. "No. Men manage wickedness quite fine on their own. . . . Don't dwell on brimstone, Boy. We've bigger problems at present."

With that, we entered the convent.

12 ⁖ Thievery

Oh, was this convent fine. It included the church, of course, an infirmary, a winery, a buttery, a hostel for pilgrims, a finer hostel for wellborn ladies . . . even a badge seller with lead badges in the shape of a veil.

We walked through the church to a chapel screened by iron bars, a chapel guarded by a hawkish nun. Within the chapel rose an altar as tall as three men. Pilgrims knelt, clutching their vials, and gazed at the top of the altar, at a crystal chest on a shelf. Inside the crystal chest, barely visible, lay a yellowed piece of linen.

Secundus knelt, but his eyes stayed on the nun.

I knelt, and watched, and waited. The tear-soaked veil was so high! My knees began to ache. "Do we ask the nun for the veil?" I whispered. She did not seem very nice.

"Shh." Secundus bobbed his head to the nun, then led me into the darkest section of the church, the dark so dense that it made me fearful. He reached into the neck of his robe and pulled out a key—a small rusty key on a cord. The key stank of rotting turnips, rotting eggs, foul air. . . . At once I realized 'twas the key that made Secundus smell so sour. The key and the book.

He gazed around: no one observed us. He unlocked a door and nodded me into a small chamber.

I recoiled in horror: Stone coffins flanked the walls!

But Secundus only locked the door behind us. "Don't fear. These folk will not mind our company." He pulled out his candle stub, and by its light settled into a corner.

"But milord, 'tis not—" The truth hit me. "You're going to steal the tear-soaked veil!"

"No, Boy. *We* are going to steal it."

"I am not a thief!"

"Indeed you're not. But don't you want to help the wife of the Castle of Gold?"

"Yes, but—"

"The nuns will not help her. Nor her husband."

"But . . ." I pondered. "We cannot steal it. 'Tis locked behind a screen."

Secundus grinned, and held up the stinky key. "Behold, Boy: the key to hell. The key to hell picks all locks."

"What? How did you—" I tried to find the words. "Does *he* know you have it?"

"You mean Satan?" He snorted. "He's too slothful. Sit, Boy. I will tell you a story. A legend I heard from a man. A man who had once been pope."

"You knew a pope?"

"I've known several. And he told me—don't look so surprised."

"You knew a *pope*?"

"Will you shut your mouth, please? This pope told me a legend. A legend about Saint Peter. Peter, you know, holds the key to heaven and stands at heaven's gates."

"He has a curly beard. Father Petrus told me."

"Ah. Yes. The pope told me that if someone brought all the relics of Peter to his tomb in Rome—if someone gathered all of his pieces in one place—then Saint Peter would open the gates of heaven. So I have made it my business to learn everything I can about his relics. To identify where they are, and how they can be . . . found. Rib tooth thumb shin dust skull tomb. Guards, you know, can be bribed, or tricked. But locks—locks need a key."

"The key to hell." The very words made me shiver.

"Yes. I must get to heaven, Boy." He coughed, and for some time he could not stop. "You see," he gasped, "my time is short. I am . . . not well."

He did not say more, and neither did I, and for hours we sat whilst the candle guttered and I pondered the nature of sin. Stealing is wicked, yes. But Secundus was trying to get to heaven. That was good—yes? Was it wicked to help a woman have a baby? Father Petrus would say no.

Was it wicked to wish to be a boy instead of a monster?

Far above our heads the bells rang lauds, marking passage from one day to the next.

Secundus stretched. "Are you ready, Boy?" He stared at me. "Boy?"

I nodded. A single, small nod. I would steal for him. I would do something that sometimes is wicked because I must help my master, and I must help this childless wife, and most of all I must get to Rome.

The church was dark now but for the candles burning at the altar of the tear-soaked veil. We approached, my heart hammering—

Secundus froze.

Behind the locked screen knelt a nun. A nun guarding the altar.

What would we do? We could not get past her—

A noise reached our ears: a wheeze. The nun was snoring.

Secundus's lips twitched. He looked at me, and up at the veil. I shook my head—but already he was unlocking the screen.

Oh, I did not want to do this. But I must become a boy.

So I tiptoed around the nun, and with fingers and boots began to climb the altar that was as high as three men. *Do not tip over, altar,* I prayed. *Do not squeak.*

Up I climbed, slipping on the smooth marble . . . but not slipping much. I did not fall. The nun snored on.

What you're doing is sinful, I scolded myself. But another thought came to me, too, a wicked thought: *This is also a little bit fun.*

I reached the shelf with the crystal chest holding its yellowed relic. *Do not think of this as fun, Boy,* I scolded. *This is serious. This is life and death.*

I glanced down: Secundus stood watching.

I reached. I opened the crystal chest, and withdrew the veil, thanking Saint Peter.

I latched the chest shut, slipped the veil into my tunic, and began to descend.

A soft click.

The chest fell open.

The nun stopped snoring.

I froze. *Do not wake up, nun.*

The nun grunted, and scratched her face: "Dearie me . . ."

I peered around, panicked: Secundus was nowhere in sight!

"You've dozed off," she muttered. "What if they found you sleeping again?" She fussed with her habit, straightening her sleeves. She looked up.

I clung, halfway down the altar, my eyes as wide as a rabbit's.

The old nun squinted. "Dearie me, what is that?"

I did not move even a muscle. But oh, the candles burned bright.

The old nun lumbered to her feet. "No," she whispered. Her rheumy eyes traveled up and down my body. My blue tunic. My face. My hair.

No, thought I, trying so hard not to blink.

"It cannot be . . . I must tell the others." She fumbled in her robe—stared at me—and shuffled off, shooting me one last glance. "Sisters," she cried, doddering through the church. "Sisters, I have seen an angel!"

13 ⋰ Thumb, the Third

We were out the front door of the church before the old nun
creaked out the back. Secundus knew of a door in the convent's
walls behind the buttery, and oh, how I at that moment appre-
ciated the key that picks all locks! Then we ran, the ripening
moon lighting our way. I feared brigands, yes, and wolves, and
I feared the dark very much; but at that moment I feared nuns.
What if they caught us? What if they found the tear-soaked
veil so carefully hidden beneath my tunic?

Soon enough the church bells rang—warning bells,
different from the bells marking prayers or celebrations. The
jangling prompted me to hurry still faster, my breath ragged
in my ears.

Secundus cocked his head: hoofbeats approached! We dove

into a ditch, and watched through weeds as a rider galloped past—a rider from the convent.

My heart clenched in fear, but Secundus laughed. "He is riding to the Castle of Gold, Boy. Soon the wife will know that the veil has been stolen."

"But that is terrible, milord!"

He grinned. "'Tis perfect. By the time we arrive, she'll be ready to barter."

We did not meet any more riders, though I jumped at the cries of night animals and even at birdsong, and checked again and again the veil tucked beneath my tunic and belt.

Day brightened, and ahead rose the Castle of Gold, glowing in the pink of dawn. How pretty it looked. Like a story.

"Play your part, Boy, and kneel when you should." He wiped his brow. "This hour will determine my destiny."

A crowd as noisy as starlings filled the castle courtyard, everyone twittering about the theft. Secundus wandered, listening with both his ears.

Two boys eyed me, snickering. My dratted curls . . . At least they paid no notice to my hump beneath the pack of Saint Peter. Blessed Saint Peter.

"Come, Boy," cried Secundus. He was with a man, a sharp-faced steward in formal dress who glared at me. He led us into the castle, to a staircase, and along a dim hall.

Secundus squared his shoulders.

We entered a room. What a room! Milady's chamber in paradise must be as fine as this. Marble covered the floor, and glass covered the windows. A candle burned even in daylight. Paintings hung on every wall. . . .

Beside me Secundus knelt. The steward knelt. Only then did I perceive the woman praying before a gold-bedecked altar.

I fell to my knees, my eyes busy beneath my lashes, and at length the woman finished her prayers and came to us: the wife of the Castle of Gold. She was adorned in gold from head to toe: gold netting held her brown hair, gold flowers were stitched into her gown, gold decorated her long pointed shoes.

We bowed—I bowed as I had been taught—whilst the sharp-faced steward whispered to the wife. She bade us to rise. The cross on her chest had a crystal panel; within, I could see, lay a fragment of bone. "Behold those curls," she cooed at me.

Secundus beamed. "The boy is as honest within as he is handsome without."

"Even as a hunchback?" asked the sharp-faced steward.

I flinched. That word I had not heard in days, and it felt like a slap. A slap and a stone. *I must go to Rome to become a boy.* I would kneel before the tomb of Saint Peter, and touch my hand to the tomb's wall, and all at last would be well.

"Hush," the wife chided her steward. She turned to Secundus. "Now. You have the veil, I believe?"

Secundus's eyebrows rose. "My lady, I know not of what you speak."

"Enough of that," she chided. "What might interest you?" She gestured to her altar. A gold foot stood upon it, and gold arm—both doubtless holding bones. Yellowed bones glowed inside glass vessels, and the candlelight twinkled on vials of oil and blood.

Secundus examined them. "I seek one relic in particular. A relic from the pope himself . . . The thumb of Saint Peter."

The wife stiffened. "How do you know of this?"

He smiled. "I hear many tales."

"That relic was a gift for freeing Jerusalem from the infidels,

given to my great-great-great-great-great-great-grandfather."
She did not stumble whilst listing the greats.

Secundus smiled a smile of ice. "I heard his skill lay mostly in slaughtering helpless infidel babies."

The room fell silent. The wife's lips went white, and her cheeks. "How dare you."

Secundus smiled. "So. The thumb."

The steward leaned forward. "First show us—show my lady—the veil."

But Secundus only smiled.

The wife scowled, tapping her fingernails against her rings. She turned to the steward: "Get it."

The steward took her arm. "My lady, you are a woman, and women can be weak of mind. Do you appreciate the hilt's priceless value? At the very least—"

The wife shook off his hand. "You are *my* servant, and the hilt is *my* dowry. Bring it to me this instant, and address me only with respect."

The steward bowed his head, but his lips were tight, and slowly did he remove a box from beneath the altar, and slowly unlock it. Within the box lay the hilt of a shattered sword. Scraps of leather yet clung to its grip.

Secundus reached for the hilt—and jerked back. He smiled, and nodded to me.

I knelt before the wife—knelt as I had been taught—and pulled the tear-soaked veil from beneath my tunic. I proffered it as respectfully as I could manage.

"Where is the chest?" the steward demanded. "The crystal chest?"

Secundus spoke to the wife: "Is it a chest you want? Or a baby?"

The steward flushed. "But—my lady—how can we even know this rag is the veil?"

"Of course it's the veil, you clod head." She lifted it: "I will have a child! This year!"

"Take the thumb, Boy," murmured Secundus.

The steward glared as I reached for the hilt. 'Twas so heavy that I grunted—strong men indeed had wielded this sword. Imagine a knight pounding into battle, protected by the thumb of Saint Peter!

"The *thumb*," Secundus repeated. Now I saw a wee door in the hilt, a door to a compartment holding a thumb's knuckle bone.

"My lady—" the steward tried, his voice hard . . . But he stopped when she flashed him a look, the veil clutched to her heart.

The hilt I left in its fine carved box, but the thumb bone I grasped in my fist as we left.

Oh, did the sharp-faced steward glower at us from the battlements as we strode down the hill, away from the castle. Secundus gripped his staff as he strode, but his other hand, I noticed, was shaking.

Hurriedly we made our way, changing direction often. Soon as I could, I slipped the thumb into the pack on my back. How pleased Saint Peter must be to find so much of himself in one place!

At last Secundus drew to a halt, both of us wheezing. He took out his quill and ink and book so sour. He flipped through to the list: "Rib tooth thumb shin dust skull tomb," he murmured. With a flourish he crossed off the next word: "Thumb." He showed me the page:

~~Thumb~~.

14 ⁘ A Little Boy with a Cold

We walked the rest of that day, past orchards tangled with weeds, and huts sagging with vines, and wheat fields turning to forest. The air breathed spring, and I wondered how soon 'twould be before I could give up my boots that by now were more holes than leather, and walk as God intended, with His earth between my toes.

A noise reached my ears: a quiet but persistent quacking. I peered about but saw neither duck pond nor ducks. Secundus marched with a straight face. Too straight.

"Milord, were you . . ." Such an odd question! "Were you making duck sounds?"

"Me? Never." But he could not help smiling.

Soon we were exchanging all sorts of animal noises—cows

and doves and pigs and goats, horses and swallows and cats, larks and geese and hawks. When 'twas my turn again, I could think of no animal, so I moved my mouth but said naught and declared I was a butterfly, which made me laugh and Secundus smile.

Secundus pressed his lower lip over his upper, and blew into his nostrils.

"What are you doing, milord?"

"I am an animal. Guess."

"That is not an animal, begging your pardon."

"Ah, but it is. 'Tis an elephant."

"What is an ephelant?"

"An *elephant* is a beast the size of three horses with a gray hide and a nose longer than you are tall."

This was too ridiculous even to laugh at, so I did not.

"'Tis true. They come from the East and are useful in battle. Were useful."

I tried to picture a giant dark horse with a Boy-shaped nose . . . but I could not. So I said, "Click bukka-bukka doo."

"And what is that?"

"That is . . ." I thought. "A peekybush."

"And what is a peekybush?"

"'Tis . . . 'tis an otter with the head of a snake, and it climbs roses to sing for its supper."

"Ah. Well, do you know twee-baat-baat-baat? That is a giant swallow with feet like a man's, and it tries to land on branches but always falls off."

"Because of the feet!"

"Yes," he answered solemnly. "Because of the feet."

We continued in this fashion till my belly ached from laughing.

Secundus glanced at me. "You sound like my son."

At once my giggling stopped. *Secundus has a son?* "You—you have a son, milord?"

"Yes. Though I try not to think of him, because it hurts. He . . . left, many years ago. As did his mother. My wife."

Secundus has a wife? Although he would have to, would he not? For it takes two souls to make a child. And sometimes also a tear-soaked veil. "You have a wife?"

"Yes. Flavia. Lucius . . . I have not spoken those names in an eternity."

"Oh, milord."

"He ran everywhere. I don't think he ever walked. Till one day he got a cold. A little boy, a cold . . . We sent for physicians. Learned men—not like today. But he died."

So much sorrow in those three words.

He stared into the distance. "We mourned him. We buried him. And then I buried her. But they did not go to hell."

"I . . . I am so sorry. I am glad they did not go to hell."

"Yes. So am I. *They* were not sinners."

"You are not a sinner, milord."

"'Tis kind of you to say. But I committed many sins. I protected the strong instead of the weak. I defended the rich from the honest claims of the poor."

"You defend me, and I am the weakest person I know."

Secundus did not answer, however, for his eyes were far away.

We came to a wet spot in the road, and had to pick our way. Songbirds trilled from their nests in the reeds, and far overhead kestrels cried. But I paid little notice to all this, for my head was aswirl. Secundus had a son! A son and a wife whom he missed very much. How awful to lose a child and a wife. . . . I thought of Sir Jacques. Poor Sir Jacques. He, too, had lost his family. I must pray he finds peace.

That night we camped in an empty barn—what a funny life I had. One night in a bed all to myself, the next beside coffins, and now this shed with gaping roof.

I said my prayers as always, adding extra prayers for Sir Jacques and for Secundus's family. Secundus studied his book, his pilgrim badges catching the light of his cook fire.

A rustling.

Secundus reached for his staff. I stiffened.

Through a gap in the wall waddled a quartet of geese. They glared at Secundus with yellow eyes and snapped at him as they passed. They stood before me, nipping each other.

Secundus began to laugh.

Hush, hush, the geese snapped at him. *We all of us think you're too loud.* And at me: *We all of us think you need to make room.*

What choice did I have but to lie down?

Two geese settled on my chest, and two on my legs. *We all of us think you're too skinny,* they complained, their heads already under their wings.

"I have heard of goose-feather blankets," said Secundus, "but I have never heard of a blanket of geese. How do you do it?"

"I don't know. They simply show up."

Hush, hush, ordered the geese. *We all of us think you're disturbing our sleep.*

"Good night, milord," I whispered.

"Good night. You are something, Boy. You climb altars and serve ladies and now you sleep beneath fowl."

"Thank you, milord." *And thank you, milord, for telling me of your son.*

15 ⋅⁙⋅ Trouble

The steward was standing over me—the terrible sharp-faced steward from the Castle of Gold. "You're a hunchback," he taunted. He held up his hand in the sign of protection, and his hand, I could see, was made out of gold. "I am watching you," he whispered, and he kept his eyes on me whilst biting off his hard gold fingers. His eyes, too, were fashioned from gold. . . .

The geese were gone when we awoke, and I lay shivering at this image of the steward, willing myself to get up. The wind blew chill as we left the barn, and the clouds hung low and gray. I heard no birdsong but only last year's oak leaves yet on the branch, rattling like bones.

A trouble-filled day, this would be.

As we walked, we passed men struggling to move a cart

loaded with a single great cheese, and women doing their best with a flock of pigheaded ducks, and a shepherd dragging a sheep into a town.

'Twas a market day, though poorly attended—so cold that even beggars were absent—and housewives had a good trade in hot wine. The few peddlers huddled around a fire. The wind cut through my tunic. I rubbed my arms, missing my goatskin, however much it stank, and wishing that the pack of Saint Peter could warm the rest of me.

"Relics for pilgrims!" cried a relic dealer. He pointed to Secundus's hat. "I've a badge for you, I'm sure."

Secundus cast his eye across the man's table.

I wanted the warmth of that fire, I did. But I waited as a servant must.

"I've the blood of Saint Thomas that will cure any wound. Dust from the king's private chapel. Water from the River Jordan." The dealer waved a gold-flecked feather. "I've an angel wing!" The quill was dark with dried blood.

"You've wasted your gilt on a goose feather." Secundus coughed as he scanned the table.

"I've a saint to help with your cough, I'm sure—"

"I am fine," Secundus snapped. "I'm unused to cold air, that is all."

My eyes played over badges from two dozen shrines, palm leaves from the Holy Land, fragments of bone beneath glass. Oh, would Father Petrus delight in this. He taught me all about saints and relics and symbols. A small box glowed—a brass box half the size of my fist.

I peered closer. I longed to hold it, for the box seemed to warm the chill from the air. A pig was scratched on its lid. Curious: I did not know pigs had saints.

Secundus strode away. "Come, Boy."

"Yes, milord." I could not take my eyes from the box. "That is a very fine pig. . . ."

"Pig!" scoffed the relic dealer. "'Tis a drawing of a key. Within rests a relic of Saint Peter."

Secundus stepped back to the table. "What did you say?"

"Centuries ago wicked Saracens attacked the city of Rome, looting even the tomb of Saint Peter. One infidel stole a fragment of the saint's toe. His family preserved it, thinking that someday it might make their fortune. A monk on pilgrimage to the Holy Land heard of this toe—"

"And begged to see it, and kissed it, and carried it off in his mouth." Secundus yawned.

"What? How did you know this?"

"Half the relics in Europe have this selfsame history. If I had a coin for every monk who bit off a piece of saint, I'd be rich as a king." Secundus reached for the box—and jerked away.

The relic dealer pursed his lips. "You blaspheme, sir."

"Come, Boy. I am weary of haggling." But Secundus did not move.

"You may have that box for three florins," offered the relic dealer.

Three florins? A florin is the price of a sheep! He wants three sheep for a wee brass box?

"Three florins for that?" Secundus raised an eyebrow. "I liked it better when it was a pig."

"Two florins."

"Fine." Secundus tossed the dealer two thin gold coins. "Take it, Boy."

I picked up the box, and I am sorry to report that the scratched image looked very much like a pig and not at all like a key. I bobbed thanks to the dealer and followed Secundus, the box warming my hands. A relic worth the price of two sheep!

Secundus wove his way through the crowd, dodging peddlers and chickens and puddles, and soon enough we were back on the road, the cold wind in our faces. "Put that in the pack," he ordered, glaring at the brass box. He snatched out his book. "How did I miss it?"

"Miss what, milord? 'Tis grand, is it not? We just found the toe of Saint Peter."

He spun at me, his eyes fierce.

"I do not need the toe! 'Rib tooth thumb *shin* dust skull tomb.' No toe! Seven. That is the perfect number. Not eight. Where have I gone wrong?"

He marched, nose in his book, so I was left to my own thoughts. Again and again I dwelled on the image of Secundus tossing the relic dealer the coins. My master had two florins in his purse. Two florins, when honest men toiled all their lives without ever laying eyes on such wealth. 'Twas not proper for a pilgrim to carry gold. It made me right uncomfortable.

The air warmed as dusk fell, and in the east the clouds broke to reveal a glorious full moon. We came upon an abandoned church. The doors were gone and much of the roof, but still, it was shelter, and the dark corners did not frighten me so much, for church shadow is different from shadow outside.

"What have I missed?" he murmured for the thousandth time, shutting his book. He settled against a wall. "Let me see at least what is in that pack, Boy."

With some effort I untied the knots on my chest. Ever so carefully I laid out the relics:

A fragment of rib, wrapped in black velvet marked with the lily of the king of France.

The tooth from the abbey of Saint-Peter's-Mount, wrapped in silk the color of sun.

The thumb bone from the Castle of Gold.

A yellow toe bone in its brass box marked with a key (or a pig).

"Rib," Secundus spoke. "Rib, tooth, thumb, shin . . . That should be a shin, that one. Not a toe."

"Rib tooth thumb shin," I whispered, "dust skull home."

"Why can you never remember? 'Tis not *home;* it is *tomb.*" He glared at the box. "I do not like this at all. Put them away, Boy. This does not bode well."

I returned the four relics to the pack, settling the toe bone in its wee brass box, and wrapping the thumb in the sun-colored silk with the tooth. How fine the velvet was that cushioned the rib. The lily of the king of France. However had Secundus—

The truth hit me like a blow.

Overwhelmed, I curled up in a corner to think.

Secundus's voice drifted across the floor. "I ought to have made further inquiries. . . . No, that source couldn't be trusted. . . . Perhaps the greedy fool in Avignon will know. . . ."

I should comfort Secundus—tell him that finding the toe of Saint Peter meant his quest was blessed. That Saint Peter wanted us to find it.

But I could not, because I was too busy pondering his florins.

Too busy pondering the rib from the chapel of the king of France—wrapped in velvet marked with the king's own seal.

The key to hell picks all locks—so Secundus had told me, and so I had witnessed. He used the key to hide us in the nuns' church, and to unlock the chapel of the tear-stained veil, and to escape from the convent. He had stolen the shoe in Saint-Peter's-Step, to trade it for the tooth in the monastery.

How had Secundus acquired the rib of Saint Peter? There was only one explanation. He must have stolen it in Paris, using the key to hell.

He stole those florins.

However in the world did my master acquire this key—a key that verily stank of brimstone?

Perhaps, my mind whispered, *perhaps Secundus is a demon.*

Stop, I ordered. *Do not even think this.* And I squeezed my eyes shut and clutched the pack of Saint Peter, and whispered every prayer I knew to make that thought go away.

16 ⁙ Angelus

Ox was chasing me. He was chasing me with hounds.

Dogs love me, I tried to explain, but somehow I could not, and instead ran in panic, crashing through bushes as hounds bayed on my trail. Hunt, hunt! they cried. Bloodlust filled their barking and their words. We smell him!

Wake up, I ordered myself. 'Tis only a dream. Wake up, Boy. Awaken—

I woke to a nightmare worse than a dream.

Moonlight flooded the ruined church in which we'd taken shelter. Outside, hounds barked madly. Horses whinnied, and steel clinked against steel.

I leaped up, clutching the pack of Saint Peter—I must flee! But the church had no other exit, and the walls were too high to climb.

Secundus faced the doorway, gripping his staff.

How I wished for shadows. But the clouds had cleared, and the moon had moved, so the dark church was lit bright as day.

The hounds burst into the church: *Hunt, hunt!* they cried. *Kill!*—for hounds on scent go somewhat mad. They leaped at me—

I pressed into the corner as the hounds, desperate to attack, bayed round me.

"Back," cried a huntsman striding in, whip in hand. A hunting horn hung from his belt, and a knife. He cracked his whip. "Back!"

The hounds flinched at the sound. *Hunt!* they cried, quivering to lunge.

A second man entered, wielding a sword. He stepped forward—and he was upon Secundus, his sword at Secundus's throat.

Secundus did not flinch and his grip on his staff never wavered, but neither did he move.

The hounds leaped. *We found him, whip man! We followed the scent on the veil!*

Do not hurt me, hounds, I pleaded.

The hounds looked at the huntsman, confused. *He speaks, whip man. Hunt?*

A third man entered the church. This man I knew. I had seen him not two days past—the sharp-faced steward from the Castle of Gold. The man who in my dreams snapped his fingers for gold. He approached Secundus. "You," said he. "The relic thief."

Secundus regarded him. "I did not steal your lady's relic. She gave it to me in trade."

Whip man, whip man, what do we do? cried the hounds.

"Yes," sneered the steward. "But you stole the tear-soaked veil. And I've learned from a certain relic dealer that you stole the toe of Saint Peter."

Oh, were the hounds loud. I could not hear above their racket. *Please, hush!* I begged.

Secundus frowned. "I did not steal the toe. I paid two florins for that miserable bone."

The small one speaks! the hounds cried. *Hunt kill?*

Please don't kill me, I pleaded. *Though I know that you could. You're fine hounds.*

"Two florins?" the steward scoffed. "You and I both know

what that relic is worth." He nodded at Secundus's purse, his voice oozing with greed. "Give me the toe."

We're fine hounds, he said! bragged the hounds to one another. *We're fine, said he, said he!*

You are. Shh . . . I strained to listen over their baying.

Secundus gazed at the steward. "No." He spoke calmly, even with a sword at his throat.

The hounds' barking softened. *We're fine, he said—did you hear? Did you hear?*

"This boy's got a bag of some sort," called the huntsman, eying the pack in my arms. "Away, hounds! Away!" He cracked his whip.

Do not snap, whip man! snarled the hounds. *We hate it, that whip!*

"Bring it to me," ordered the steward.

"No!" I cried, cowering.

No, no! cried the hounds. *The small one is frightened!*

The huntsman stepped toward me. "You heard him."

I gripped the pack tighter. They could not take Saint Peter!

The hounds whirled and bayed. *No, no! The small one does not like you!*

"You little—" the huntsman reached for me. He grabbed my fine blue tunic—

Hunt! howled the hounds. They leaped at him—

The huntsman jerked back—

The tunic ripped. Strong, the cloth was, but worn, and the huntsman's grip was fierce.

The tunic fell off my shoulders.

Never reveal yourself, Father Petrus had ordered. But revealed I now was.

In horror and shame I fell to my knees. "I'm sorry, Father," I whispered, the pack of Saint Peter clutched to my chest. "I'm so sorry."

I huddled, my head bowed. The night air prickled my hump.

Silence . . . and in the silence, a thud. The huntsman dropped his whip. "No!" he screamed. He ran, pounding across the floor and into the night.

I shivered from fright and cold. *Hounds, can you hear me? What is happening?*

The hounds pranced in confusion. *You spooked the whip man,* they marveled.

I didn't mean to! Oh, did the silence unnerve me. I turned to Secundus. "I am sorry, milord, for revealing myself. . . ."

Secundus stared at me with wide eyes.

The swordsman gaped, his arm slack. He looked at the wall behind me and swallowed. "Angelus," he whispered.

The sharp-faced steward stared, too, his eyes never leaving my hump, and his face blazed with greed. He licked his lips, and drew his knife, and took a step toward me.

Secundus eased away from the swordsman, and quick as a wink swung his staff at the man. Wood met skull with a crack, but still the swordsman kept his eyes on me as he fell.

The steward spun at Secundus, knife in hand. "The thing is mine!"

"Don't hurt my master," I cried. *Don't hurt him!*

Don't hurt him! echoed the hounds. They leaped, for dogs prefer action always, and as one they lunged at the steward: *Don't hurt his master!* The largest hound bit the steward.

The steward dropped his knife. "Cursed beasts!"

Hunt! snarled the hounds. They circled him, growling.

The steward turned and ran, the hounds on his heels baying *Hunt, hunt! Hunt, kill!*

Pounding hoofbeats—the horses bolted away. Still the steward ran, hounds baying after him.

Moonlight lit the church. My ripped tunic on the floor. My skinny hose-covered legs.

I swallowed.

Secundus stared me. The swordsman lay unmoving at his feet.

"Master . . ."

"Don't speak to me!" He held out his staff. "Tie on the pack. Now!"

And so I did because I knew naught but to obey. With shaking fingers I tied the pack to the end of the staff, Secundus hissing his impatience as I knotted the cord.

At last the pack was secure. He snatched the staff, and headed for the door, staff in hand.

"I am coming, milord." I scrambled for my tunic—the fine blue tunic, now so torn.

"You are not!" He glared at me, and the wall behind me. He stepped through the doorway, the moonlight framing him, and he was gone. Gone with the pack of Saint Peter.

"Milord!" I stumbled past the swordsman sprawled unconscious. I looked about—

The east wall, so shadowed when first we arrived . . . Now the moon lit every square inch.

The wall had suffered from vandals and time. But above the altar, a section yet retained paint. An image of someone with curls and wide eyes, and a hump twixt its shoulders. Two humps, in fact, far bigger than mine.

Not humps.

Wings.

Faded though this image might be, there was not a shred of a doubt 'twas an angel.

III

Deceit and
Calamity and Ruin

17 ∴ One Thousand Years of Devising

"No!" My scream echoed around the church. I scrambled for the ripped tunic. It covered me—somewhat. I needed the pack of Saint Peter! I needed it to protect me till I reached the tomb—

My master ran away when he saw me. When he saw my hump.

The huntsman ran screaming, and the swordsman collapsed, and the sharp-faced steward called me a thing. *The thing is mine,* he'd said, licking his lips.

An image came to me: the angel feather of the relic dealer. A goose feather it had been, dusted with gilt—but the goose had bled to produce it.

I dashed out of the church, clutching the flaps of my tunic. Cow muck ripped off my boots but I did not pay heed. "Milord!" I ran, my bare toes gripping the earth.

The thing is mine, the steward had hissed, the moonlight glinting on his knife. . . .

Now I understood, finally, why I must never reveal myself. If folk ever saw my hump, I would be as dead as that goose. I'd be cut into a thousand pieces and sold on the steps of every church in Christendom because some greedy fool thought my hump made me an angel.

Desperately I peered, seeking Secundus, whilst also glancing back—was I pursued? The sun mounted the horizon. *Do not shine on me, sun,* I prayed. *No one must see my hump. My hump that is—no, no, no!*

A fox barked: *Beware: someone comes.*

There he was. Striding as fast as ever, his staff with the pack on his shoulder.

"Secundus," I called. Oh, my relief!

"Stay away!" He glared at me, and past me.

I spun—but there was naught behind me but dawn.

Secundus shifted his grip on the staff, blowing on his fingers. The staff must be hot, what with the relics tied to its end. "Stay away!" He recommenced walking.

I followed. I did not know what else to do. I was so feared

of the sharp-faced steward. So feared of being called angel or thing. For all his rage, Secundus seemed to have no interest in slicing me up. And he journeyed to Rome. Where I must go to become a boy. Naught mattered but that.

We traveled some distance in silence, the sun climbing its way up the sky. Never did he pause, and never did I. Oh, I tried not to think of my hump, nor of the angel on the church wall. The swordsman whispering *Angelus,* so stunned that he crashed to the floor. The steward hissing *The thing is mine* like a miser counting coins. . . .

A harsh laugh: Secundus. "An angel. Just my luck."

"I am not an angel!" I cried. "I am Boy—"

He turned upon me: "Truly? Tell me, *Boy:* do you eat?"

Like a slap, this question was—so fierce I stepped backward. "No," I whispered. 'Twas true. I did not eat. But this was a truth I did not like to dwell on.

"You take my food. You take honey."

My cheeks burned. "Father Petrus said to take food when it's offered. The dogs love it so. . . ." *Everyone's different,* Father Petrus had said. *You'll understand someday.*

"Do you urinate?"

I did not know that word.

"Do you piss?"

I hung my head: No. I pretended. Father Petrus taught me to.

"What have you got between your legs?"

Always tell them you're a boy. . . . "Naught, milord," I whispered. How awful I was.

"What? I cannot hear you."

"Naught." That was my secret—my most horrible secret. I was a monster with no boy parts, with no parts at all. That was why I must reach the tomb of Saint Peter.

"Ah." Secundus gritted his teeth. "Angels do not eat or drink or piss. Angels have no . . . they've naught between their legs." He glared at me. "You're an angel, you dumb fool." Off he strode, blowing on his hands.

I scuttled after him. *I'm not an angel,* I wanted to shout. *I'm a monster who wants to be a boy.*

"I said to stay away," he hissed. "If men discover what you are, they will kill me, too."

"They won't—" But the memory of that sharp-faced steward . . . he'd have killed Secundus to get to *the thing.* He broke his own fingers for gold. . . .

"I cannot die! I cannot die *yet.*" Secundus snatched out the key—the dark stinky key. "How do you think I acquired this? How do you think I know beyond doubt that my wife"—his breath caught—"that my wife and child are in heaven? How do I know?"

I didn't know. I didn't want to.

"Because I come from hell!"

I leaped back. "You're a demon! I thought so—"

He barked a laugh. "Don't be daft, you stupid twit. I'm a *sinner.* I am a man—I was a man. A man who sinned and died, one thousand years ago. Who one thousand years ago was damned to hell." He pressed his knuckles to his lips. "Flavia," he whispered. "Lucius." He began to cough. He coughed so that he had to lean on his staff. "No one escapes hell unscathed," he whispered.

A noise behind us. Baying. Hounds approaching, fast.

At once I ran. I had no choice. I ran like the prey that I was.

Secundus ran, too, faster even than me.

The hounds were upon us, baying madly. The hounds from the church.

Secundus spun, shaking the pack of Saint Peter from his staff. He crouched—

I crouched—

The hounds tumbled over one another. *Hunt, hunt!* they cried. *We found you!*

Secundus swung at them. "Get away!"

The small one! the hounds laughed, leaping about me. *Hunt, hunt—you're here!*

Secundus glared down the path. "Where are the men?"

Where are your masters? I asked as the hounds wriggled, licking my hands.

The whip man cannot track the scent! they chortled. *And the other has too sore a paw.*

I puzzled over their words. "I think the huntsman is lost, and the steward is hurt."

"What? How do you know this?"

"They—" *Never reveal yourself.* "They . . . told me. The hounds did."

"They told you?" Secundus looked rightly suspicious. "They *barked* it?"

"No. I understand them, that's all. And they understand me." *Can't everyone talk to animals?* I'd asked Father Petrus, who had chuckled and patted my curls.

Secundus's eyes narrowed. "Ah. Because you're an angel."

"I'm not an angel! I just can."

Secundus studied me, and the half-dozen hounds at my feet. Bloodthirsty hounds, now as docile as doves, grinning as I scratched their ears . . . "Can you talk to any dog?"

I shrugged. "Dogs like me." The hounds lolled in bliss at my scratching.

He tapped his chin. "You want to go to Rome, yes?"

"Yes, milord!" I must become a boy.

We found him, we found him, the hounds boasted to one another.

"There is a man—a man with whom I must negotiate. For the shin."

Oh, yes. Rib tooth thumb shin . . .

"He has a dog." Secundus waited.

"Oh. And you—you think I can talk to the dog?"

"Can you?"

"I don't know. I've never met him."

Secundus's eyes hardened.

"But I can try."

He stared at me. At the hounds . . . and off he set. Just like that. Striding along with his staff. "Get the relics," he ordered, pointing to the pack he'd dropped. "And hurry. *Boy.*"

"Yes, milord." I did not mind if he said my name coldly. Not if he took me to Rome. Right quick I retrieved the pack of Saint Peter. How nice it was to hold him again.

The hounds sniffed. *What have you there?*

Something good. But not food.

"Hurry, I said," called Secundus.

Quick I tied on the pack. It hid my hump, and the cords held down the torn flaps of my tunic.

The hounds trailed us, yipping in glee. I must follow Secundus, because he was my only hope of becoming a boy. Even though he was a thief. Even though . . .

That man smells of farts, stated a hound.

He smells of bad eggs, said another.

No, no, bayed a third. *'Tis old turnips.*

On I trotted. *You're all wrong,* I told them. *What you're smelling is brimstone.*

Brimstone? A big brown hound butted my hand. *What is that?*

I scratched his ears. *Brimstone is the smell of hell. 'Tis hell that my master stinks of.*

18 ⁑ Downstream

Rocking is the word for the motion of a boat. But it's a false word, for a boat does not rock like a cradle, no; it quakes like a witch shaking a baby. I did not want to sit in a boat with naught but a shred of wood betwixt my bottom and the bottomless deep. But 'twas our only solution, for the river flowed faster and straighter than ever we could walk.

All that morn we had trekked away from the ruined church and the awful night within it. The hounds leaped round my legs, delighted with the adventure, baying *Rabbits!* and *Hunt!* and *Me, too!,* and I listened so I would not have to think of anything else.

At noon we found the river, a river half as wide as the sky, and the hounds sniffed out a tiny boat beneath a pile of branches. *Hunt, hunt!* they bragged. *Men hid this!*

"What are you doing, milord?"

Secundus tossed the branches aside. "I'm getting us where we need to go, *Boy*." He pushed the boat into the water. "Get in."

The hounds leaped about: *Hunt! We found it! What now?*

Across the river stood a huddle of buildings—and a huddle of men shouting at us.

"Silence those hounds," Secundus ordered, "or I will." He settled in the boat the size of a wine cask. Waves smacked its hull like claws wishing to drag us to death.

Such fun! bayed the hounds. *We can swim!* They leaped into the river.

"Get in, I said," Secundus snapped. "Or should I leave you behind?"

The thing is mine, the steward had said. . . . Shivering, I stepped into the boat. How it rocked. I gripped the sides with both my hands, and tried not to look at the water.

Secundus pushed off. The hounds swam around, baying. "You're bringing them with us?" he asked, incredulous.

"I'm not—'tis not my decision. They want to come."

"If they follow us, they will drown." He began to row.

Oh, I did not want them to drown. But I did not want to lose them, either, for then I'd be alone with naught but a wasps' nest of thoughts. *Hounds,* I cried, sadly. *You must not follow us.*

What? they answered. *No hunt? But we're fine! You said so!*

Yes, I did—and you are. But 'tis not safe. My heart sank, saying these words. *You should find your kennel, and your keepers. And your pups.*

Ah ... our kennel. Our pups. One by one, they turned to shore, though a few ran along the riverbank till they, too, peeled off, and followed their own trail back home.

Good-bye, I cried. *Good-bye, friends.* And then I had naught to think of but my own unhappiness, and the misery of this wee small boat.

The rest of that day we floated. We passed cliffs and villages. We passed rafts of barrels and rafts of sheep, and ferries with horses tied behind, swimming. I'd think *I will drown* when the boat rocked, or *I will vomit* ... although I had naught to puke for never did I have food in my stomach. Did angels even have stomachs?

You are not an angel, I scolded. *Even though you do not eat, and have a hump on your back, and the gift of speaking to creatures ...*

Whatever I was, I must get to the tomb of Saint Peter in Rome. I must become a boy.

Secundus rubbed the scar on his palm—the burn he'd received from the rib of Saint Peter. He caught me watching. "One thousand years will do that," he said coldly.

"Do what?" I did not understand.

"Relics—true relics—drive away demons. I've spent enough time in hell, it seems, that relics also drive away me." He frowned at the scar.

"Do . . . do relics burn other men?" I asked, thinking. "Or only warm them?"

Secundus snorted. "Why? Do they warm you?"

Hastily I shook my head, which set the boat rocking. *Wicked you!* I chided myself. *'Tis wicked to lie.* Relics did not warm men. They only warmed . . .

I am not an angel, I scolded. *Stop talking, mind. I'll no longer listen.*

The sun drifted toward the western horizon.

"Behold." Secundus jerked his chin.

I roused myself to follow his gaze. Downstream stretched the longest bridge I ever did see. It had a span as long as an arrow's flight, and stone arches that crossed the river like stitches in cloth. Beside it rose a city with dozens of spires. The riverbank was crowded with ships, their masts a straight black forest. Shouts drifted across the water like smoke.

"Rome," I breathed. "Now I can become a—"

Secundus snorted. "You think this is Rome? 'Tis the miserable city of Avignon where the pope now cowers. He fled Rome—you did not know?—because Romans today are a murderous rabble of villains. Here we must recover the shin. The fourth relic—" His face grew dark. "The relic I'd thought was fourth. It appears I know less than I'd fancied."

Recover? I did not like the sound of that word. "Milord, I do not wish to steal."

"The shin of Saint Peter belongs at his tomb in Rome. We must return it."

That sounded better. Return is what you do with things that are lost.

Our boat drifted toward the forest of masts. Secundus steered with his oars. "Stay close to me," he warned. "Do not get . . . found."

Do not get found. . . . I shivered.

Our boat bumped against a pier. "I have met more souls from this place than I can count," Secundus murmured, and with that he leaped ashore.

I followed him. Into Avignon, to *return* the shin of Saint Peter.

What a city it was. What a cesspit. Tall buildings made narrow streets even tighter, and hammering assaulted the sky. Palaces rose from the ruins of houses. The streets were clogged with beggars, and finely dressed women, and servants clothed from the wealth of their masters. Men wore strange and foreign caps and helmets. Perfumes battled with stench, the smell worsened by piss pots emptied from windows, by candle smiths boiling tallow, by the spent grain of brewers being gobbled by pigs.

"Hurry, Boy. I have men to bribe. 'Twill take time to locate the man with the dog."

A rich man clothed in red strode toward us, guards clearing his path—

Around the man's neck hung a pendant displaying a fragment of bone.

I hunched, quaking with fright. *What if that man thinks I'm an angel? I will be chopped into one thousand pieces! My teeth will be pulled from my head, and my fingers ripped off. . . .*

"Move!" Secundus followed my gaze. "Ah."

The man in red drew closer. His guards were almost upon us.

With a hiss Secundus dragged me into an inn. "I should like a room for this one," he announced to the inn wife scrubbing the hearth.

The inn wife snorted. "You'll not find a bed in all this town. The whole world comes to the pope."

Secundus displayed a fistful of coins. Coins he'd stolen, no doubt, but I was in no state to object. "I said I should like a room."

"Well now." The inn wife wiped her hands. "I've an attic. . . . It's small, mind you."

"So is he." Secundus jingled the coins. "He need only be safe."

Her eyes on the coins, the inn wife led us up stairs smelling of onions, and other stairs smelling of cats. She stopped at a rough door with a rusted padlock that she unhooked to reveal a dark attic cluttered with broken benches and a chest.

"There's bedding"—she nodded to the chest—"and a piss pot. I'll bring dinner—"

"Do not worry yourself." Secundus touched the rusty padlock.

"We've lost the key, I'm afraid—"

"'Tis perfect. In with you, *Boy.*" He dropped coins into the inn wife's hand.

She eyed me—my curls and pack and ripped tunic. Quick I ducked away from her prying.

The door shut behind me. "I will come for you," Secundus called, "when I need you." The padlock snicked shut.

"What's that?" The inn wife's voice rose. "How do you have a key to this lock?"

Footfalls: Secundus walking away.

"I said, how do you have a key? Answer me. Answer me, pilgrim!"

I took a deep breath. "I will be safe here," I whispered into the darkness. "I'll be safe."

Safe from men craving relics, perhaps . . . but would I be safe from the thoughts inside me?

19 ·:· Newly Hatched Chick

The attic was not totally dark, for light leaked through a broad gap below the door. Standing on the least broken of the benches, I opened a shutter that revealed naught but a wall. Open was better than closed, however, even in the dusk, and it aired the attic. The chest revealed ancient bedding that I spread on the floor, stacking the benches to one side. The piss pot I left. All my life I'd been baffled by men's pissing and squatting. *That is one mystery solved,* said the voice in my head: *Everyone pisses but angels.*

Hush! I scolded—but had not time to think more, for something was scratching its way under the door.

The something turned out to be a cat, mottled in gray and orange. She purred when I stroked her, and curled up on the bedding. 'Twas quite like the goat shed, this attic, though I had blankets here instead of straw, and a cat to chat with instead of goats.

We talked of mice, the cat and I, and of the importance of napping. When it became too dark to see, I sealed the shutter. I said my prayers, praying that Saint Peter protect me from harm, from Ox's stones and Cook's scolding, from the sharp-faced steward who called me a thing. . . . I shivered.

The cat kneaded my arm. *Mmm, come. Let us rest.* I settled beside her soft furry body, the pack of Saint Peter warm on my back, and her purring lulled me to sleep.

The steward was looming above me. He clinked his fingers together—fingers now made out of knives. "Angelus," he hissed, gold eyes glittering. "Monster. Thing . . ."

I jerked awake. "No!" I cried. "I am not any of those—"

The cat curled against me. *Mmm,* said she. *Come back to sleep. . . .*

Her purring woke me the next morn—that, and an odd gurgle outside.

Cautiously I opened the shutter. A stream of rain fell past, from a gutter carved into the shape of a monster.

"I am not a monster," I whispered, remembering my dream. But the gutter monster did not care, nor did the cat. The steward was far away. I need not fear his knife fingers.

I watched the gutter spewing rain. I had naught else to do.

Cat? I asked. She flicked an ear. When I petted her, she turned away. *Play with me,* I begged, but she answered *mmm* and kept sleeping.

I poked at the benches too broken to fix, even if I'd had skill and tools.

Avignon, thought I, *is not at all interesting.*

My hump itched.

Had my hump ever itched me before? I could not recall. Although I could never recall being so idle. No dogs, no goats, no Father Petrus, no Secundus. No Ox, even, hurling insults and stones. I missed Cook! She'd at least find me something to do.

The bells of terce rang for mid-morning, the finest bells I ever had heard.

Now I must wait for the church bells at noon.

Noise wafted up from the street—laughter, and someone selling something I couldn't quite hear.

My hump itched.

"Stop itching," I grumbled. "You have never itched before. I cannot scratch you."

And why not?

Because *never reveal yourself.*

But I had revealed myself—the huntsman had revealed me for that one awful moment (*don't think of that, Boy*). I must keep myself covered or I'd be chopped into bits (*don't think of that, either*).

My hump itched. Oh!

What exactly is your hump? my mind asked me. *I'm curious.*

'Tis not to be touched, I answered. But oh, it itched, and now my mind itched, too—naughty curiosity! This attic was safe, and I was alone. No one could see me through the window. The empty hours loomed before me.

So—shameful me—I determined to discover the truth of my hump.

With guilty fingers I untied the knots of the pack, and set it aside.

The ripped tunic fell from my frame. I stood naked but for my hose.

With a deep breath, I reached for my hump. I scratched it. I *felt* it.

Soft the hump was, with bones inside the softness, small bones that tucked this way and that. Pinfeathers covered my skin, like the wings of a newly hatched chick.

"I am not an angel," I whispered. But again I reached, and again I touched feathers and bones. Muscles I never had known moved in my chest. Muscles along my spine.

With great courage I grabbed at the hump and stretched it. From the corner of my eye I could see the feathers all greasy and limp, each feather as short as my fingers.

The cat yawned and stretched and settled herself. I held out my hand. She sniffed it, and wrinkled her nose.

The wings—I mean, things—did not smell . . . did they? What if men could smell them, and find me?

I must clean my hump! But how? How did one clean wings—er, hump—when one hadn't a beak? I did not even have a bucket or bowl—

The piss pot!

Gagging, I held the chipped piss pot under the rainspout. Soon enough I had a pot of fresh water. I found a rag in the chest, and went to work.

Oh, was it hard, for my arms were in front and the hump in

back, and my wings—my whatever they were—had no strength at all.

Perhaps angels groomed each other, like a cat with her kittens . . .

I offered my back to the cat, but she turned away. Cats.

I dumped the piss pot out the window, and filled it again and again, scrubbing my hump that had never been touched. Soon the room stank of wet fowl.

Angels can be quite revolting.

I scrubbed and rinsed till I shook with exhaustion. How I felt for wee chicks just out of their eggs.

A noise touched my ears—someone was coming! "I'm sorry, dear boy," called the inn wife. "We've been so busy—you must be starved." She pushed a bowl of stew under the door.

"Um, thank you. You are too kind."

I fed the stew to the cat who curled her tail around her toes as she nibbled, and I collapsed onto the bedding, as sore as though I'd been haying. I pressed the warm pack of Saint Peter to my hump. The two things were damp. How to dry them? Birds dried their wings by flapping. Perhaps . . .

My chest spasmed, and my back.

Angels are useless, I thought—and immediately *I'm not an angel!*

I am not an angel, I repeated as I worked the things attached to my shoulders. But every time I moved them and washed them, the word crept closer, till by twilight I called them by name. *I have wings,* I thought as the vespers bells rang. *I have wings, and I even can flap them.* And I could, though every movement made my chest burn. Exhaustion slapped me harder than Ox ever had, and with great effort I sealed the shutter and fell into bed.

Cook opened the attic door, and strode in scowling. "What a mess you've made," she snapped. "Look at you lying about." She reached for the covers.

"No!" I cried, pulling them tighter—

But she yanked at the bedding. "What are you hiding, you lazy thing?"

"I'm not hiding anything," I lied—

"I'm not—!" I cried, jerking awake. Was Cook here—?

Of course not. 'Twas only a dream.

I curled, catching my breath. What if Cook saw my wings?

Mmm, the cat murmured. *Stop moving. . . .*

I awoke the next morning aching like a very old man. My wings—oh! they were larger, and every feather fuller. Every time I moved them, it seemed, they grew, and whilst I could now extend them somewhat, I could not draw them in. Not enough. What if someone saw me? Not Cook to be sure—she was far away, and so was the steward. But others had eyes. The inn wife, for example . . .

So I tore the washrag to ribbons, and with much grunting tied my wings down, feeling quite like a trussed chicken. It hurt, but my pain was better than others' attention, and with time (I hoped) I would notice less the pinching and tightness.

My wings could scarce bear it, however, and they ached as legs ache when one crouches too long.

When the inn wife brought food again, I begged for a thread and a needle, and repaired as best I could my ripped tunic, and donned it over my wings. Then, when I could stand it no more, I removed my tunic and untied the rag ribbons. Such relief! My wings spread as wide as my elbows. How fine it felt to stretch them.

Mmm, said the cat. *You flutter, but you're too big to eat.* She went back to sleep.

At dusk I sealed the shutter, and tied my wings down. However much they loved to be free, I could not risk exposure. What if someone came in whilst I slept? I wept at the pain, and put on my tunic, and tied on the pack of Saint Peter. The warmth of Saint Peter at least helped the ache.

I nestled beside the cat, who stretched, making room. *Mmm. You look silly,* she said.

I hope I don't. I hope that I look like a boy. I petted her, and she purred. But I was not a boy, and would not be till I reached Rome. I had wings I must hide or they'd cost me my life.

I sighed.

Mmm. The cat curled her tail over her nose. *What is it?*

O cat! I swallowed. *I must confess it: I think I'm an angel.*

20 ∴ Kicked in the Shin

A shock of cold air—Cook tugging my bedding—

"Wake up!" A light blinded me—

Secundus stood over me. "What have you done, you dumb pail of milk? Your hump is bigger!"

"I am sorry, milord!" I nigh wept in shame, tugging at my hose and tunic and pack.

"Come. Hurry." He strode out of the attic. I hurried to follow.

The cat curled up in the spot I had left. *Who'll be my bed warmer, mmm?* she asked.

You'll be fine, cat—and I'm certain she was. She at least did not have to tiptoe through the inn, and wince as Secundus unlocked the front door. A cough racked his body, and in the

166

lantern light I could see his flushed cheeks. In three days he'd visibly sickened.

He jerked his head at me: Hurry.

'Twas the depths of night. Avignon's streets were as quiet as tombs, and as dark. Secundus shielded the lantern. "We meet the man with the dog. You can control the dog, yes?"

Control? I talked to dogs. Sometimes I made requests and they agreed, but that was not controlling. I could barely get the cat to wake up. "I'll try."

"You'll succeed. And you may have to climb into a pit . . . don't shiver."

But I could not help it.

We climbed cobbled streets. Before us rose a palace as big as a mountain, with a gate as high as a tree. Cook would swallow her tongue! Through the gate came a carriage with four horses, with guards fore and aft, and a messenger running behind.

Secundus led me through the gate into the largest courtyard I ever had seen. He slid through a shadowed doorway into a corridor, handing me his lantern. He redoubled his grip on his staff. "Ah. Here he comes, with his hellhound."

A man approached, a man with a face like a vulture, dressed half in black and half in red, with shoes twice the length of his feet. Behind him paced a dog the size of a pony. His pink eyes drooped, and his massive jaw hung loose.

The dog is not from hell, I reassured myself. *He does not smell of brimstone.* But oh, was the dog frightening. *Hello,* I tried, the lantern trembling in my hands.

The dog curled his lip, revealing long teeth.

"Pilgrim," greeted the man—Lord Vulture, I shall call him. Wickedness flowed from him like a very bad odor. He sneered at my hunchback beneath the pack. "Come."

We walked. Behind us slinked the dog.

Hello, dog. I have friends like you back at home.

The dog sniffed at the pack of Saint Peter, his breath chilling my neck.

The lantern sent awful shadows dancing against the walls. *Hello, dog . . .*

No answer.

Laughter drifted toward us. "You are missing a fine party, my lord," said Secundus.

"They are too drunk to notice my absence." Lord Vulture

seemed to float in his long shoes. The dog's nails clicked on the stone.

We reached a door.

Lord Vulture looked at Secundus, and at the door's lock. "You have the key?"

Secundus nodded, not moving.

With a sigh of disgust Lord Vulture turned his back.

Secundus unlocked the door—so quick that I barely smelled the brimstone, though the dog growled. He stepped back so Lord Vulture might lead.

The room within—oh, 'twas fine. Tapestries hung on the walls, and three candles (three! in a room that was empty!) set twinkling the stars painted on the blue ceiling.

"Guard him," Lord Vulture ordered the dog, nodding at me.

The huge dog circled me, sniffing.

Hello, dog, I tried again. *Why won't you talk to me?*

Lord Vulture gestured to the bed: "Beneath that." And then: "You are not even pushing," for it took all of his strength and all of Secundus's to move the heavy oak.

All the while the dog sniffed me. His jaw brushed my bare toes, leaving a trail of cold saliva. I tried not to tremble.

At last the bed was moved.

Secundus counted the stones on the floor, and set his staff into a crack. He pried up a long stone, and Lord Vulture propped the stone up with his sword.

The dog sniffed my hand.

That is cat, I explained. But I feared that what the dog smelled was angel.

Secundus nodded to a pit in the floor—a pit half as deep as me. It held small bulging sacks, and a small chest sheathed in gold. "In with you, Boy. Get the shin."

Lord Vulture rubbed his hands.

I eased myself in. 'Twas like a grave, that pit. The dog watched, drooling, and Lord Vulture seemed almost to be drooling, too.

"Hurry," prodded Secundus.

I reached for the chest. 'Twas cold to the touch. Cold . . . I shot a look at Secundus. A look—naught more. But that look was enough.

"Hand it to me." Secundus took the chest without a wince. "Get out," he ordered.

With great relief I did so.

"Back in with you!" Lord Vulture shrieked. "The sacks!" The dog snarled.

"It is fake!" cried Secundus, hurling the chest aside. He kicked the sword free, and the stone crashed down.

Lord Vulture leaped back—but the dog was behind him so he could not leap far, and the heavy stone fell down, down . . . onto the tips of his too-long shoes.

"Kill them," screamed Lord Vulture. "Kill them both."

Secundus snatched up the sword. "The relic is fake, you swine!"

The dog snarled, and snapped at the air.

"Attack," cried Lord Vulture, struggling to move his feet. But he was right stuck. By his vanity was he pinned to the floor. "You stupid beast, tear out their throats!"

Again the dog snarled and snapped. But he bit the air. Not Secundus. Not me. The dog turned to me and spoke one word—one word only—and spoke it only once: *Run.*

"Milord," I cried. "We must run!"

"Attack!" Lord Vulture demanded. He smacked the dog, whose snarl deepened.

"The lantern, Boy!" Secundus leaped past Lord Vulture into

the hall, and I followed. He slammed shut the door. "You're a liar," he shouted through the wood.

Voices—a distant cry—

He kicked the door. "I needed that bone!"

"Milord, we must depart." The shouts were closer, and the glow of torchlight.

"That was the fourth relic! *My* relic!"

"They are coming. If they find us—" I gulped.

"For decades I've planned this!" Again he kicked the door. He stomped away. "Come, Boy. We go this way, and turn left, and then right."

The directions at least were not lies—not like the words of Lord Vulture—for they led us to a storeroom filled with bolts of cloth, and a door hidden behind the bolts—a door that Secundus of course could unlock. The tunnel beyond stank of sewage and rot, and looked darker even than night. But I followed, shaking with fear, and I nigh shrieked when he stopped to study his pages.

"The shin," he muttered. "Rib tooth thumb shin—*shin*! Now what?"

Who cares? thought I. *Naught matters but escape from this tunnel. We've relics enough—* "Milord!" my voice echoed. "The toe!"

"What of it?" he snapped. "Hold the light closer."

"The toe is a relic. Rib tooth thumb toe—does not that work instead? The shin might be fake, but the toe is real."

Secundus lowered his book. "You have a point."

I did my best to sound calm. "We have four relics. Saint Peter has seen fit to aid us."

"Rib tooth thumb toe . . . I shall have to ponder this."

Onward we trudged. I tried not to dwell on what squelched betwixt my bare toes.

The stench shifted from sewage to fish; the air freshened. We came to a grate. A quick whiff of brimstone as Secundus unlocked it, and we were on the banks of the river, the sky pink in the east. Sailors shouted, and water splashed, and the bells rang prime to mark the morn.

"Hurry." Secundus pushed his way along the riverbank, studying each ship and sailor.

A shout behind us. "Stop them!" I heard . . . or I thought that I did.

A ship was pushing off. "We need passage!" cried Secundus.

"Won't have it," returned the ship's master. "Heave, men."

Another shout, closer . . .

"Five florins," cried Secundus.

The ship's master paused. "Ten."

Secundus leaped aboard. "Come, Boy." Already the ship was three feet from the dock. "Jump!"

Behind me a trumpet sounded. "Stop them!" a man cried. I knew that voice!

Dropping the lantern, I ran—I leaped for the ship—

Secundus grabbed me with his hand so scarred from the relic. With a grunt he hauled me aboard.

"Milord!" I nigh shook him, I was so feared. "The steward's behind us!"

21 ∴ At Sea

I will never forget that awful voyage. I've feared many things in my life: Brigands. Wolves. Cook. Night. The sharp-faced steward who trailed us. But now I feared sailors.

Oh, were they superstitious—of women, birds, sounds—but mostly of me. They made the sign of protection right to my face, and muttered that I was a monster. Never had I felt so alone. I'd rather suffer Ox—at least on land I could flee.

Secundus, for his part, did not believe I'd heard the voice of the steward. "That scoundrel is halfway across France!"

So I said no more, though my mind dwelled on the steward's shouts of "Stop them!" and my dreams of him breaking off his own gold fingers, and clicking his fingers like knives. . . . whilst Secundus cursed his luck because he so hated sailing, and muttered over cups of the ship's vile wine.

The ship carried wool to the cloth merchants of Florence—bales of wool filled with mice. The mice, too, were rude—nigh as rude as the sailors—and even the gulls were unhappy. They complained that the land was too close or the land was too far, and chided me for not giving them food. When I explained I did not eat, they flew off in horror and never spoke to me again, but floated over the ship, gossiping about me, and mocking.

On the ship sailed, lurching with each swell, though the sailors claimed the weather was fine, and indeed blamed me for the wind. "The hunchback's luck will make us pay later," they grumbled, and laughed when I gagged at the rolling.

How long each day was, and each minute. Once Secundus bellowed my name, and I climbed over the wool bales to where he sat tossing dice with the cook. "Hold this," he ordered, handing me the ink pot, and opened his book to the list. "Rib tooth thumb shin dust skull tomb," he read aloud. "Shin," he repeated, hissing, crossing it out with thick lines of ink. Beside it he wrote another word—"Toe," he murmured—and crossed this out, too.

~~Toe.~~

"Congratulations, milord," I said, and for the first time onboard I smiled.

His face darkened as he flipped through the pages. "Dead ends," he muttered. "What else have I missed?" He downed his drink and recommenced dicing, and I slipped away, my happiness gone.

That night I poured for him as he sat with the sailors, dining on fish long dead. The sailors recited tales of bloodthirsty pirates, and mermaids who drew men down to hell.

Secundus laughed till he coughed. "And what of it? From hell, you simply escape."

Escape hell? scoffed the sailors. 'Twas impossible.

"'Tis not," slurred Secundus. "'Tis only very hard. I will tell you. First you go to hell—which all of you'll do, I wager—and you befriend the damned. You befriend even Satan, because Satan needs good counsel. Are you listening?"

"Of course," a sailor laughed. "I need to if I'm going to hell."

"That you are . . . You learn everything you can. And you wait. You wait centuries. You wait till pestilence strikes the world. Millions of souls, pouring into hell. Too many to count. And you stand—are you listening?—you stand in this river of souls. You step closer—just one step—to the gates. The next day, you step again."

"That'd take forever!"

"It takes years. All the time, you fear you'll be found. You fear pestilence will end. But at last you reach the gates—the gates that always stand open. You pocket the key to the gates." He chuckled. "No one will notice its loss. Then you're free."

The sailors shifted, eying each other. "Does your master always talk such nonsense?" one asked me.

'Tis not nonsense. He comes from hell, this man does. But such words would end both our lives. Instead I shrugged. "You should hear what he says of the English."

The sailors roared in relief, and Secundus stumbled off to vomit, and the next day his cheeks were gray though the sweat of fever gleamed on his forehead.

Still the sailors watched me, and glared. *What's in it?* they'd ask of the pack on my back. *What riches? What does his hump look like, I wonder* . . . till I feared even to sleep. So I resolved to find somewhere safe far from them, and from the mice that complained I stank like a bird.

What a fool I was.

That night I climbed the rigging, and settled on the long straight yard that holds up the sail. The clouds hid the stars and the moon, and the night air felt as soft as a cloak.

Somewhere above me a goose honked, and another goose answered.

You are up late, geese, I called.

We know, they answered. *We are all of us headed to nest.* Their honking faded, though I fancied I could yet hear their wings. What would that feel like, I wondered, flying through the soft night air?

Stop, I scolded. *You must think about sleeping.*

My wings ached. Always they ached, but up here they ached more. I had not stretched them since the inn in Avignon, and oh, they throbbed. I must release them—

No! 'Twould risk my life, and Secundus's. And stretching seemed to make them grow.

But the notion would not give me peace. I was alone. No one could see me. I would stretch only till the pain eased. 'Twould only be a moment.

And so I fell to temptation.

Carefully I removed the pack of Saint Peter and tied it to

the mast. I removed my blue tunic, and tied it over the pack. I unbound the rag ribbons that held down my wings.

At the first movement, my wings cramped—such agony!

The pain passed, and—oh, joy!—I could spread them. The salty breeze licked me like a dog's warm tongue. My wings cupped the air as hands cup water.

I stood on the yard. That is how brave I was: I stood as I once stood on trees, my arms spread wide, and my wings, and never in my life had I felt such delight.

I balanced on that yard for I do not know how long—balanced and bobbed and skipped and danced. How delicious, how perfect, it felt! At last common sense scolded me to stop. So with great reluctance I sat, and went to work settling my wings.

But the wings wouldn't obey.

I cursed them for being so stubborn, and myself for being so stupid. When I did manage to tie them down, oh, how they hurt. But suffering was my punishment for prancing midair, and so I bound them, weeping, and donned my tunic, and the pack of Saint Peter, and I tied myself to the mast to sleep.

The sun found me cramped and shamed, but with joy in my

heart . . . till I returned to deck, where the sailors looked at me in horror, and as one made the sign of protection.

My curls were no worse than ever; the pack sat as always on my hump. . . .

Secundus loomed over me. "Your hump is bigger. What have you done?"

"Naught, milord—" which was a lie.

"Keep out of sight. The sailors are frightened enough."

And so I did, and did not free my wings again no matter how they ached. I sat by Secundus as he drank and muttered, the wind blowing us to Rome, and I slept so close to him that I smelled his key to hell. I'd dream of spreading my wings, the breeze tickling my feathers . . . then the dream would shift to Ox's sneer, and Cook's scolding, and the hiss of the sharp-faced steward.

I'd awake with my hump throbbing in pain, my throat raw from the brimstone, and pray that this journey would end.

22 ∴ The End of the World

At last we reached the port of the city of Rome: a river of thick yellow water clogged with shipwrecks and reeking of swamp.

With great effort and cursing by the crew, the ship drew up to the bank, a bank that had once been grand but whose stones now tilted madly or lay half buried in muck; few walls remained standing. The people, too, looked worn and cracked. Beggars clustered around Secundus but stayed far from me, and all made the sign of protection. Secundus hissed at me to stand up straight.

One beggar, his arms tucked beneath filthy rags, insisted on guiding us to Rome.

"I know the route," Secundus snapped. "I lived here."

But the beggar trailed us, saying it was a full day's walk to the city, and unsafe due to brigands.

Secundus picked his way along streets that were now rubble paths. The houses lacked roofs, their insides choked with weeds. Pestilence, I knew, left buildings empty but standing; warfare burned them to the ground. But these houses had suffered so slowly that even the ghosts were withered to dust.

We passed two men smashing pink marble walls.

"That was a house of pagans, fine pilgrim," whined the beggar.

"Shut it," snapped Secundus, his lips a thin white line.

We approached a pit that glowed like hell . . . though (I told myself) it did not smell of brimstone, and the men around the pit did not look like demons.

"They harvest pagan stone," the beggar whined. "The rich pilgrim like to see?"

A man hurled a rock into the pit—a rock carved like the head of a woman, her hair held in place with a band. Between the coals glowed a great muscled torso.

"God's work to make limestone . . ." The beggar kept his

eyes on Secundus's purse. "To build churches for greatness of God."

"That is not limestone, you barbarian. That is art." Secundus wiped his eyes. "This city, Boy . . . I had a friend here I'd visit. His family imported wine. We'd sit beneath his pomegranate tree and quote the poets, sampling the best of Spain and Sicily and Provence, in crystal glasses . . . 'Tis hard to imagine, I know."

No. 'Twas impossible.

The land turned to marsh as we walked, the road raising itself out of the mire. Ahead stood a tower ten stories high—a tower that a magpie would make, with many colors of marble, and columns mismatched.

"Brigands, pilgrim," piped up the beggar. "They build tower and call themself noble. From everyone they take money."

Secundus stared at the tower. He looked across the marsh to distant columns sticking up like bones. "I was warned. But I could not believe it. . . ." He reached into his purse. "Go away," he said, tossing a coin at the beggar.

The beggar shot out an arm. He had no hand! Only a stump.

The poor man! "I am so sorry—" I began.

But the beggar scuttled off, gesturing rudely. A hunchback,

it seemed, was even worse than a one-handed beggar.

Secundus trudged toward the ramshackle tower. "Come, Boy."

Men appeared, men with scarred faces and ragtag weapons.

"Brigands," I breathed, my heart beating.

"Poor pilgrims got fat purses, eh?" the biggest brigand smirked. His black beard was a tangle of curls. "What's the boy got in his pack?"

A girl elbowed past him—a girl no older than me, with filthy feet and tangled black hair, though she had a jeweled lady's knife in her waistband, and red ribbons in her curls. Her eyes were black and quick and hard.

She studied me. "Uncle, he's not a boy."

Secundus clinked a fistful of coins. "Forgive me, but we need to pass."

At once the brigands turned toward the clinking—

But not the girl. "What are you?" she asked me, as a farm-wife tells a hen *you'll be lunch*.

"I'm naught—I mean, I'm a boy—"

"He's my servant." Secundus added a coin to his palm. "We have just left a ship where he terrified sailors because sailors find hunchbacks bad luck. In Avignon we sought the pope, but the pope himself was feared, because of the bad luck that hunchbacks will bring."

The brigands shifted, and stepped back.

"Then why do you keep *him?*" the girl asked—emphasizing the last word.

"Because I promised his mother I would. Because he says little and eats even less. Because I learned long ago never to touch his hunchback or even his pack because bad luck at once would befall me." He stepped forward. "May we pass?"

The big brigand snatched up the coins, making the sign of protection. But the girl watched with hard eyes.

Did we trot away quickly from that ramshackle tower! Secundus mopped his brow. "That girl had eyes like a serpent's. Did you see her?"

"Yes, milord." I shivered. "She scares me."

"I should think so. She'd scare Satan himself."

"Ho there," the girl called. She was following us! "Why do you pretend you're a boy?"

Oh, she made me squirm! Nervously I tested the cords of the pack.

"What do you carry?" she called. "It must be precious because you fuss. Is it gold?"

Secundus spun at her: "You think you're clever, don't you?"

"I know I am," she answered. "I'm the cleverest person I know."

"Then be a good girl," he snapped, "and go back to your hideous tower."

In a flash, the girl snatched up a rock and hurled it at him. "Don't call me good! I am wicked. Do you understand me?"

I gaped at her. Why would anyone boast about wickedness? That itself was wicked!

"My great-grandfathers were senators—do you hear? Someday I'll be queen of Rome."

Secundus snorted. "Rome doesn't have queens."

Again he had to duck. "Not yet!" the girl shouted. "But it will. And my sons will be emperors and popes. How much gold do you carry?"

Secundus strode off, his chest rattling as he breathed.

I willed myself to follow him, doing my best to ignore the wicked girl behind us. The hot Roman sun beat down. Great cracks split the ground. Broken white tombs lined the roadside, each tomb filled with bubbling green water. And a massive building on the horizon—

"Milord," I breathed. "A church!"

Secundus's face brightened. "The church of Saint Paul. Ah, Boy, we almost are there."

"Rib tooth thumb toe dust . . ." I counted. "Dust is next."

"Yes. The dust of Saint Peter, stored within the grave of Saint Paul."

Still the girl followed us! "By the way, you two are mad to travel alone."

She no sooner spoke than a howl drifted toward us.

"Do you hear that?" she chortled. "Those are wolves. They eat pilgrims."

A second howl. I shivered.

Secundus drew close: "Can you control wolves, Boy?"

I looked at him in horror. *Wolves?*

"That's why pilgrims travel in groups," the girl continued. "Why, I know of pilgrims dragged off whilst sleeping. . . ." But I did not hear more because I stomped to drown out her words. Soon enough I could make out a line of pilgrims approaching the huge church. . . .

Secundus smiled at the sight. "They are walking from Rome. We are less than a league from the city, Boy. We need only this dust, and then we will enter Rome itself—"

The girl tossed a pebble at my head. "You! Talk to me."

Secundus gritted his teeth. "Will you—will you be a *wicked* girl and leave us alone?"

"For a florin," she retorted.

"No!"

"You needn't yell. . . ." She looked at me. "You don't have to hide, you know. You can just be a girl." Her eyes drifted toward the church. "Be careful in there. The monks, they . . ." She shook her head and turned, heading back to the ramshackle tower.

"They what?" I asked. It seemed important, what she was saying.

She grinned at me. "If they catch you stealing, they cut off your hand."

23 ∵ Scrabbling

I trailed Secundus, numb with horror at the girl's words. They cut off thieves' hands! I'd seen it—the poor beggar! What had he stolen? It could not be more valuable than the dust of Saint Peter.

"Milord?"

Secundus slapped a mosquito. "What?"

"Milord, is that what will happen to us?"

"What? Ah. Do not think about such things."

You do not answer me. "Milord, I do not want to lose a hand."

"Neither do I."

That still does not answer me. "Milord, I don't want to thieve."

"Don't worry. At the moment I need a strong back and a slow mind, and you have neither."

We approached the church of Saint Paul—a massive church surrounded by old cracked buildings. The first Christians (so Father Petrus taught me) built this church directly over Saint Paul's grave, and they placed half of the body of Saint Peter beside him so that the church was doubly blessed. This was the dust Secundus sought: the dust of Saint Peter in the grave of Saint Paul.

Closer we drew to the walls lit by the sunset—so close that we were now in the line of pilgrims. Seeing me, they made signs of protection, and pointed me out to their children.

Oh, was I tired of this. I was tired of other folks' stares, and their gestures. Tired of fear.

"Cannot you walk faster?" Secundus snapped, and "Stop hunching!" He groaned. "Fine. I will store you somewhere." He flipped through his book: "No . . . no . . . Ah. Perfect. They all died of pestilence." He stopped at a door. With a twist of his wrist, he unlocked it. "Get in," he ordered. "And keep the pack safe." With that, he sealed me in a room that smelled of dust and loneliness, and held only a high empty window.

"Milord!" I called. "I must get to Rome!"

No answer.

I sighed. Oh, I loathed this! How much longer till I could live like normal folk without being glared at? How much longer till I did not have to fear the sign of protection, or knives, or the sharp eyes of wicked girls? *I go to Rome to become a boy.* Well, Rome was only one league away. . . .

And so I resolved: I would take myself to the city of Rome and the tomb of Saint Peter, and see my miracle granted. Then I'd help Secundus complete his quest. Once I was a boy.

There.

But courage is cheap. Escaping this room was impossible. Secundus had locked the door, and the window I could not reach. . . .

An idea—No! I must never reveal myself. What if I were seen?

But Secundus might be gone for days. I could not remain here, waiting and fearful. I must risk the part of an angel to achieve my life as a boy.

At once I went to work, struggling with the knots on my chest. I had the same struggle with the rag ribbons, which in several places had rubbed me raw.

The first flex made me scream—oh, how my wings hurt.

Slowly they opened, wider than my two arms. The feathers were longer, too. They shimmered.

Even in my fear and haste, I marveled at their beauty. *Can you feel the air?* I asked. *I need you. Just this once.* I tied the pack and tunic round my waist. *Please, Saint Peter. Help me. And forgive me for using my wings.*

I paced to the room's far side, filling my lungs. The window was twice as high as me. But the dusky sky gave me hope. *See, wings? Aim for the sky. We must find the tomb of Saint Peter!*

I crouched, and ran with all my speed, flapping, and when I reached the wall I leaped.

I did not get far. The wall scratched my fingers, and tore my hose. My beating wings drove my face into the stone. My toes scrabbled for a purchase. With the greatest effort I reached— grabbed the windowsill—and hauled myself up.

I lay there, gasping.

Below me lay an empty courtyard surrounded by black empty windows. No movement, no sound, no candlelight . . . This whole building, it seemed, was abandoned.

Are you ready? I asked my wings.

I did not fly—oh, no. But my wings spread enough to slow

my fall, so that I only banged my knees rather than crashing.

How fine it felt to be free.

Hurry, Boy. If Secundus finds you, he'll be right enraged.

So I bound my wings, the ribbons barely reaching: already they'd grown. Naughty wings—but I'd lose them soon enough.

I donned my tunic and the pack, tugging the cords extra tight.

I crept out of the building. I must get to the tomb of Saint Peter.

I kept my head down, following other pilgrims, a small fish in the stream of the faithful. The crowd pushed, catching me up, and as one we spilled into a square—a church square half the size of the sky! How Father Petrus would have loved to see this.

Pilgrims fell to their knees, crawling forward. I joined them. How could I not?

On my knees I entered the building, in the throng of crawling pilgrims.

Oh, 'twas sad. The church's roof had completely collapsed, and its ceiling beams lay shattered. Thick grass grew in the broken floor. "An earthquake," pilgrims murmured to one another, reaching for coins to donate, and crawling forward.

I did not have a coin, but I crawled with the others, caught up in their passion. On my knees I approached the altar—an altar protected by a railing, with two monks raking the offerings. A fine lady pilgrim lowered a string into a hole in the altar. She pulled up a long strip of cloth, and kissed it. When she left the altar, other pilgrims pressed round, reaching for the cloth.

I reached, too, and I, too, murmured "Saint Paul, Saint Paul!" and I followed the others down a staircase, to a crypt beneath the altar. One wall of the crypt had an iron grill, and behind it the narrow end of Saint Paul's stone coffin. A small wood altar stood before this grill, and two monks warned pilgrims not to scratch the walls, for pilgrims will make relics of anything.

I smiled, and the bones of Saint Peter warmed my back. *Behold,* I whispered. *'Tis the grave of your friend Saint Paul. Your dust lies within—*

A hand clamped my shoulder. Hot breath scorched my ear: "I see that my angel has flown."

24 ∻ Dust, the Fifth

I jerked like a fish, but the man grasped me tight. "You ran away, you dumb pail of milk!" Secundus!

Oh, was I relieved. "I am sorry, milord—I was seeking Saint Peter—"

"Huh!" scoffed a weaselly pilgrim with battle-scarred knuckles. "The hunchback's a liar."

Secundus shook me. "You shouldn't have come here!" His eyes burned with fever and fury and—I saw now—with fear.

"What's he got in that pack?" asked the weaselly pilgrim.

"Naught of your concern. Sit in that corner, Boy. Don't move."

Cook's voice came to me: *you stupid thing, you've jumped from the pot to the fire.* Indeed I had. Now, it seemed, I was part of Secundus's thieving!

Around us pilgrims hurried away for the night. Longingly I watched them depart.

"Does he get a cut of the bounty?" asked the weaselly pilgrim.

"No," sighed Secundus. "Nor do I. I want only the dust. All the coins go to you."

At the mention of coins, the weasel stiffened like a dog on a scent.

"For a thousand years, pilgrims have come to this grave. I have seen—" Secundus caught himself. "They dropped their donations through the lid. By now there should be wealth enough to buy yourself a cardinal."

The weasel licked his lips.

Secundus turned his attention to the monks. He filled their hands with coins, and escorted them to the stairs, promising that he would guard the gravesite whilst they sang vespers. The monks departed, reluctant to leave the tomb but grateful for the coins, and eager for prayers. They promised to return soon.

Then we were alone—Secundus and me and the weasel with battle-scarred knuckles. The weasel who so clearly wasn't a pilgrim.

"Guard the stairs, Boy," Secundus ordered. He unlocked the grill.

From beneath his pilgrim robe, the weasel pulled a hammer and chisel and pry bar. The two men hauled themselves onto the wood altar.

Music floated down the stairs: monks chanting.

The weasel hammered at the end of the coffin, matching the song's rhythm. Secundus pried with the bar. . . .

The music ended. The weasel paused, adjusting his grip.

A new song began. I peered up the stairs: why didn't anyone come? 'Twas wicked, what Secundus and the weasel were doing!

Secundus toiled, sweat beading on his brow. The weasel hammered with all his might. The coffin's stone end moved with a creak. . . . It fell. Secundus and the weasel caught it, just barely, and eased it onto the floor. Secundus reached into the open coffin—and snatched back his hand. He smiled as he blew on his fingers. "Get it all," he whispered to the weasel. "Quickly!"

Grinning, the weasel swept coins into a sack.

"The dust!" hissed Secundus.

The weasel grabbed more coins. He reached further, but he could not reach all the way in. He turned to me. . . .

No! Not me! "Milord—the beggar—"

The weasel pulled out a dagger. "Get in there," he ordered.

Secundus looked at me. "The dust, Boy. 'Twill be fast."

The weasel grinned at me as he tested the tip of his dagger.

To stand on an altar—that itself is a sin! And oh, did the coffin look dark.

"Please, Boy," Secundus whispered.

"Don't beg him!" The weasel jumped off the altar, eying me—

But already I was climbing up beside Secundus. I would help him. I must.

"Thank you, Boy. Here, step on my hand—"

I could reach on my own. With a deep breath, I hauled myself into the coffin. 'Twas so dark! And dusty. My pack caught the edge. "No!" I cried—

Ow! A sharp pain to my bottom.

"Don't touch him!" Secundus snarled at the weasel.

With a great twist that tore at the pack, I pulled myself all the way into the coffin. "I am so sorry," I whispered. "I am so sorry, Saint Paul, to be inside your grave."

"Hurry, Boy!" whispered Secundus.

The space, I concede, was large for a coffin: longer than a man, and half as wide as me. But I could not sit up, and oh, was it dark. My toes and fingers felt dirt and mortar and crumbling bits, and my head cracked on the lid. The pack rubbed, the cords fraying. "Saint Peter!"—I reached behind me—but too late. The pack fell from my back.

"Boy, gather the dust!"

"The coins, you brat! The money!"

Scrabbling, I shoved everything I touched toward the opening.

"More!" the weasel snapped. Coins clinked in his sack.

A shard of bone, a scrap of cloth . . . oh, my wings ached. They strained against the ribbons.

"Come out of there," whispered Secundus—

A shout!

I jerked back. The ribbons snapped—the stitching on my tunic ripped—my wings opened!

A pounding sound—

On my hands and knees I spun. Through the open end of the coffin, I could see monks racing down the steps of the crypt. Monks!

I scrabbled to the grave's far end. *Please, saints, do not let me be seen. . . .*

A monk approached the opened coffin. Oh, was he close! He could see right in if he tried—

He bent—I could see his shaved tonsured head—he placed the weasel's sack in the coffin—he bowed his head to pray. "Amen," he finished.

Amen, I repeated silently. Even a thief can do that.

The monk withdrew, his head bowed.

I exhaled.

More monks—monks with trowels of wet concrete. Now I would be caught for sure!

They spread the concrete round the coffin's edge, keeping their eyes downcast. Not looking in. A command—they lifted the stone end, and slipped it into place.

Darkness.

A thump that shook the ground: the monks setting a heavier stone into place. Perhaps they were blocking the iron grill?

Silence.

I crept forward, pressing on the coffin's stone end. But it did not budge.

I was sealed in the grave of Saint Paul.

I am not feared of heights and I am not feared of falling, but oh, do I fear dark. Worms should live under the earth, and corpses, but not a living creature such as me. "Secundus," I whispered. "Secundus!"

How I wished I'd called to that monk! To be exposed as a thief was a horrible fate, and worse still to be exposed as an angel, but neither was so horrible as this. I'd risk my hands— my life—for the chance to live on earth instead of beneath it, unable even to sit.

But wait—the darkness was not completely dark—

The hole! The hole in the altar through which the lady pilgrim had lowered the cloth. The hole descended from the altar all the way down through the coffin lid.

Up I peered. Candlelight flickered!

A noise reached me—shuffling. Oh, how I wanted to shuffle. To stand, to jump . . . Monks might cut off my hand, but I deserved it. One did not need hands to jump.

I pressed my mouth to the shaft. "Help!" I cried.

A barked order. A thump—the screech of stone—the light disappeared. Where once I saw candlelight, now . . . naught. Had the hole been sealed?

I reached up the shaft as far as I could . . . but my fingers did not come close to the top. "Help! Cut off my hands!"

I shouted till my throat was raw. I pounded on the slab, the walls, the lid, shouted into the blocked hole. My fists bled, my knees, my head.

I will die here.

But wait . . . do angels die? I cannot starve—to starve, one needs to eat.

Again and again I felt the walls, the floor, the dirt. . . .

I will go mad. I'm mad already.

I lay there, willing Secundus—the weasel—anyone—to come. I tried to remember: a scream . . . Was it Secundus who screamed? He must be alive—he was Secundus! He'd escaped a thousand years in hell. Could he come for me without a hand? I shuddered. "Please, milord," I whispered. "Save me."

I felt about for the pack of Saint Peter, and clutched it. I knelt, my wings rubbing the lid, and I prayed. I prayed to Saint

Peter, and to his remains within this grave. I prayed to Saint Paul, and thanked him for sharing his grave with Saint Peter.

I drifted to sleep, into nightmares that I was trapped underground. . . .

Each time I awoke to discover again that my nightmares were true.

IV

Arrival

25 ·:· Red Beard and Gray

A man's voice, sharp.

A second voice rumbled, telling a story—a long story, it seemed, but the teller enjoyed it.

Now I could see the speaker: a tall man with a beard. Gray hair curled around his face and his chin; his eyes crinkled. White linen draped his frame, and he swung a long key.

"I said I've heard it before." The second man wore linen splattered with ink, and wrote in a thick book. His beard was long and red, and red hair framed his bald head.

"Mmm? About the fishbone?" asked the gray-bearded man.

"Please, brother." The writer dipped his pen.

"Your penmanship is so lovely," sighed gray beard.

"I say it again: I can teach you." He held back his beard as he wrote.

Imagine being clever enough to both write and speak whilst holding one's beard!

"I'm only a fisherman. . . . Gracious, someone is here."

The red beard did not look up. "Yes. The angel."

"Well, bless my soul." The gray beard smiled. He was, I noticed, missing a tooth. Light came from his head. From both their heads. "Hello, there."

"Hello, Father"—for Father *seemed the right word.*

"Are you an angel, though?" He frowned. "Or a boy?"

"He is the one with Secundus." The red beard blew on his ink.

Gray beard swung his key. "Ah. Secundus. The one who found the way."

"That one." The red beard looked at me through thick brows, and oh, were his eyes fierce. "Boy, there is work to be done."

I awoke facedown in rubble.

Why were my surroundings so black? I had just been in light. . . .

I felt the masonry, but thickly. My fingertips were covered in scabs—cuts from scratching at the coffin's walls, though now the scabs were almost healed.

How long had I slept?

The tall man with his curly gray beard—how kind he'd seemed. And the bald man was ever so clever. He knew how to write, and he knew Secundus, and he knew me. . . .

Saint Peter. Of course. Saint Peter with his key to heaven. The other man must be Saint Paul—Saint Paul writing the good book.

A piece of mortar dug into my cheek. I brushed it away— and found it warm to the touch. Warm not from me, but from its own power.

'Twas not mortar, but a fragment of bone.

I grasped it. At once I saw a red-haired man preaching. Whilst some called insults, others listened with both their ears, and men and women prayed.

Saint Paul's arm, this fragment was. I could even see its out-line. . . . The fragment glowed, enough for me to make out its shape, and to reveal the five fingers on my hand. I still had a hand! I could see the grime, even, worked into my skin.

I looked around: patches marked the coffin's floor, patches not quite so dark as the rest of the darkness. Nearby rested a chip of rock—no. Bone. I touched it. At once I felt the passion that filled Saint Peter—Peter, a fisherman who did not even know how to read. A scrap of linen glowed with a dull purple light. Soon as I touched it, I knew 'twas a remnant of Saint Paul's burial shroud. I clutched it and prayed.

Every fragment in this grave had a story. Every bit must be sorted.

Boy, Saint Paul had said, *there is work to be done.*

So I worked.

I started by sorting all that I could find on the coffin floor, and arranging the bits into piles. Dried mud formed the largest mound. A river, it seemed, had flooded this church. *What if the river floods me?* But I scolded the thought from my mind: *Do not think, Boy; there is work to be done.* I piled the mud in one corner, next to the pile of coins.

The bones of Saint Paul and the threads of his shroud I arranged at the grave's head.

I made my home at the opposite end, at the foot. There I gathered the relics of Saint Peter. My pack held rib tooth thumb toe, and now also the dust of Saint Peter's bones from the grave of Saint Paul. Rib tooth thumb toe dust.

My tunic served as my pillow, for the poor thing was shredded past all repair. But 'twas no matter for I did not need to cover myself, not when no one could see me.

At first I tried to ignore my wings; I'd lose them once I became a boy. But the wings so loved to be touched, and the feathers felt so fine when I cleaned them. Caged birds preen themselves, and captive hawks. So, I reasoned, should I preen as well, and I could even reach some feathers to my mouth. Though I did not care for the taste of dust, I cherished the feeling when the cleaning was done. Grooming took many hours, but in the end my wings were smooth as silk.

Within the narrow low grave, I would extend one wing and then the other, becoming ever more adept at working them. I'd even picture how it felt to fly. Imagine soaring over the manor, waving down at Sir Jacques. Would he smile, seeing me? Would the goats notice and laugh? *Stop dreaming of flying,* I'd scold myself. *Do you want Cook to see you? Or Ox? They already think you a monster!* I did not want the cruel names that folk called me. *Are you an angel, or a boy?* Saint Peter had asked. I was a boy; I was meant to be one. Someday.

Though the saints did not reappear, I was not alone, for I had the company of a mouse. How the mouse entered the coffin I never did learn, but she slept curled against my neck, and wakened me with tickling whiskers. She brought me crumbs with eager affection, and when I passed them back, she nibbled them down: *Don't mind if I do!* She'd clean her ears whilst I cleaned my wings, the two of us like two cats grooming in sunshine.

So you see that my life was quite lovely. The worst times, in fact, were my nightmares of the steward hunting me with knife fingers, or the black-eyed girl pelting me with questions and stones. . . . I'd awake panicked, though my pulse would slow once I saw darkness. No wicked soul would find me here! Then I'd preen, and arrange the dust and bones and cloth, and set the dirt into patterns. At times I fancied hearing footsteps and the chanting of hours. But those were echoes of a reality I'd do best never to think of. Instead I taught the mouse to run along my wings, and laughed at its whiskers, and tidied. There was work to be done.

Such was my existence and such, I knew, would be my existence for a very long while.

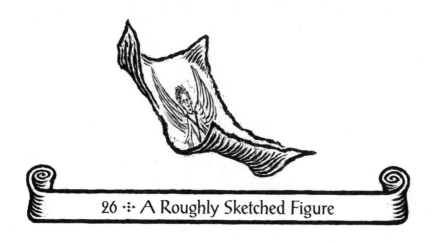

26 ∴ A Roughly Sketched Figure

Much time I spent pondering Secundus.

The one who found the way, Saint Peter called him. Saint Peter knew Secundus! That was good, yes, for Peter held the key to heaven. Perhaps Saint Peter was planning to let Secundus in. But as time passed, this hope faded, for I knew where Secundus had gone: back to hell. My prayers included a plea to Satan to treat him well. I had little faith my prayers would help, but prayer was all I could offer.

One day I was squatting in my corner with the pack of Saint Peter as always, shaping dirt into a pattern of grapevines. The mouse watched from my shoulder. I sang as I shaped, a nonsense song with nonsense verse that I used to sing to Sir Jacques till tears of laughter ran down his face. Poor Sir Jacques. I tried to sing to him after his injury, but always Cook found me and put me to work.

'Twas the mouse that first noticed. Her ears perked up.

Perhaps I should shape the dirt into ivy, which did not twist so. Had Secundus sung to his little boy? Poor Lucius, to be in heaven without his father . . .

A scrape of stone. The mouse leaped from my shoulder.

Brightness poured down through the hole in the lid of the stone altar above me. Light flooded the coffin—light so bright that I screamed. *Mouse, what is happening?* I cried.

The mouse dashed away: *Hide, Boy!*

But where? Mouse, help me!

Now could I hear arguing—odd for an altar. The light shifted. A shadow . . .

A feather floated down from the hole in the altar—the hole that now was open.

No, not a feather: a page from a book. A page with burned edges. It settled on my grapevines.

I crept over. With shaking hands I unfolded the page and held it to the light:

A sketch. A quick sketch of a boy with skinny arms and

curling hair and huge eyes. And wings. And two lines criss-crossing the boy's narrow chest . . .

'Twas a drawing of me! An angel boy bearing the pack of Saint Peter.

"Secundus!" I cried.

Shouting. A shadow passed over the hole. Voices. A crowd. A cough . . .

"Milord, I am here!"

"Who?" Perhaps *who*. Perhaps another word wrapped in the tumult. "Did I—did I hear the name of Saint Peter?" a voice cried.

"N-no . . ." What was he saying?

"You are saying we should all of us leave this church and go to the tomb of Saint Peter?"

I had not said that! But 'twas Secundus's voice. It must be. Perhaps I was going insane. . . . "Yes. You should go from here to the tomb of Saint Peter." *But do not forget me.*

Another shadow. "What are these words?" A skeptical voice, bossy.

What should I do? Should I answer? I pressed my mouth to the hole. *I hope you know what you're doing, milord.* "You should go to the tomb of Saint Peter!"

Voices like a thousand crows. The din grew, and the pounding of feet.

"Secundus!" I reached up the hole toward the light so far away. But I received only scratches and a shower of grit.

The ruckus faded.

"Secundus? Anyone?" *Mouse?* But I heard only silence.

That moment . . . that moment was the worst of my life. I had trained myself not to hope, convincing myself that life in this grave had value. But the light—the voices—had burst that hope free. Now my hope lay dashed to bits, as awful a torture as I could imagine.

I crept to my corner. Away from the hole. I curled up, wings over my ears, clutching the pack of Saint Peter.

No sound. No movement but for dust motes drifting through the shaft of light.

More dust motes . . .

Dust.

Dust rained upon my head. Dust, and mortar.

The lid of the coffin began to lift—the lid with the hole, with the altar above it. I'd seen that altar! Enormous, it was, and thicker than my arm was long. Its weight . . . I could not begin to imagine.

A sliver of daylight. A head appeared, surrounded by sunshine. "Boy, are you there?"

Bless you, Saint Peter! Bless you, Saint Paul. "Yes, I am, milord!"

"Are you—" His voice caught. "Are you sound?"

"I can hear you!"

"No. I meant—are you quite right?" The crack widened. "Can you fit through?"

How to explain? "Milord, my tunic is ripped—I can't cover my . . . things. . . . "

"'Tis heavy, Boy." Did he even hear me?

It did not matter—I must get out. So, holding the pack of Saint Peter, I climbed up out of the grave and fell on the church floor, my wings wide and drooping. I peered around, flinching at the thought of stones and knives . . . but the huge church was empty.

"Ah. 'Tis good to see you." Secundus wiped his face. Oh, did he look ill! His cheeks were hollow, his eyes bruised . . .

"Are you crying, milord?"

He smiled, and tousled my hair. "You still have the pack. Well done, Boy."

A horrific squealing—the coffin's lid was being lowered.

The lid, and the altar above it. But what man is strong enough to achieve such an impossible task?

No man. The slabs of stone were being lowered by women.

Four women. Four washerwomen with rolled sleeves, their arms muscled from four lifetimes of wringing out clothes. Each wielded a pole for stirring vats. They *tsk*'d as they worked, backs straining. . . .

The lid with its great stone altar settled back in place with a thud that rang up to the sky.

"Milord, why is the church empty?"

"Shh," Secundus smiled. "I'll tell you anon."

The women surrounded me, beaming. Stroking my hair. Holding me up. Brushing dirt from my hose. Chuckling and cooing as they opened my wings. My wings! White, yes, but blue as well, and violet, and gold, and rich red at the tips. How they gleamed.

The washerwomen folded the wings—they'd been folding since before I was born—and settled them against my body.

Oh! Wings should fold.

Images came to me: swallows tucking their wings when they

landed . . . sparrows flicking their wings back as they hopped for crumbs . . . swans gliding down onto water, settling their wings as they floated so gracefully. . . .

"What are you doing?" Secundus frowned at me.

"I am sorry, milord. I was trying to move like the birds. . . ." How fine the feathers felt against my skin. My wings wiggled like toes in a shoe.

"Hmph." He coughed. "Your hump is gone."

"What?" I spun, silly me: no one can see their own back! I felt with my hand. . . .

I had wings, yes. But wings that now rested between my shoulder blades. No hump.

I stood, stunned . . . and jumped as a washerwoman knelt at my feet. Quickly she stitched up the holes in the knees of my hose. The others held up a tunic they'd stitched in no time at all, from the lining of one of their skirts. They slipped it over my head, the linen soft and pale from years of washing. Oh, did it rest well on my back.

"How fine it feels," I whispered. "Thank you."

The washerwomen chortled, and with strong arms they tied on the pack of Saint Peter.

I tested the cords and turned to Secundus. "Rib tooth thumb toe dust. Now you have five."

He smiled. "Yes. And I have you."

The washerwomen kissed my curls and waved as Secundus and I strode off through the huge ruined church, the blue sky above us. *Good-bye, mouse,* I called. *Good-bye, Saint Paul. Thank you for sharing your grave.*

"Come, Boy."

So quiet, this church was, and empty . . . Or was it?

"Come," Secundus repeated. "We must hurry."

27 ❖ The Heads of Saint Peter and Saint Paul

As everyone knows, the bones of Saint Peter rest in his tomb in Rome—except of course for his dust in the grave of Saint Paul. But many years ago, the pope decided the two saints' heads must be preserved specially. So he took the head of Saint Peter and the head of Saint Paul, and put them in the Mother of All the Churches because that is the church of the pope himself. Thus the Church's three heads were all together: the pope and Saint Peter and Saint Paul. The pope has since fled to Avignon to escape savage Romans. But his church remained in Rome, and so did the heads of the two saints, guarded and never displayed—except for this Holy Year of 1350, when they sat on the altar for millions to see.

And so 'twas to the Mother of All the Churches that

Secundus and I trekked, walking the league from the church of Saint Paul to the city of Rome. We had rib tooth thumb toe dust, and now we needed the skull. How marvelous the sunshine felt, the breeze tickling my curls. How fine to have a back that was smooth, and the pack lying smoothly upon it. We walked an ancient road, alone but for the whine of mosquitos.

"Hello, marsh," I cried, skipping. "Hello, ruins."

"Slow down." Secundus smiled. "We've some distance to go."

I skipped back to him. "You're not dead, milord!"

"Nor are you."

"I was so worried, but you're alive."

"So you've observed."

"And you still—" I took his hand. The hand with the scar.

"No. The monks did not catch me."

The weasel—the scream . . . "Milord? How did you survive?"

"Ah. That was a scene. When the monks discovered us, I had only a moment. So I smashed my head against the wall."

"You did *what?*"

He removed his hat to display a yellowing halo of bruise. "I hit my head so hard I passed out. When I awoke, I said the other pilgrim had hit me." The weasel.

I was so stunned I stopped walking. "But—that was lying."

"Ah, Boy. I had to survive. You see, stealing relics is a very great crime. But almost worse is crime at an altar. That man was guilty—don't you agree? I simply added another sin to his list." His smile faded. "And you? How did you manage?"

"'Twas not bad at all."

He shuddered. "They would not let anyone near the grave, not for money or prayers." He tapped the key beneath his robe. "Not for small coins, at least." His smile returned. "How I missed you, Boy. The guard dogs—"

"You *stole?*"

"I stole all that I could, from every rich man in Rome! And I found strong women, and I gave the church this many coins"—he cupped his hands like an orange—"so I could get to the hole in the altar. So I might—" He swallowed. "So I could learn how you'd fared."

"I knew 'twas you! That's why I shouted."

"And I heard you. I cannot describe my relief. At once an idea came to me, and I announced that a voice said everyone must leave this church to go to the tomb of Saint Peter."

"That voice was me." I shivered in pleasure.

"Ah, Boy, you played your part well. And everyone left." He shook his head, still amazed. "Even the abbot."

What a scene it must have been. Thousands of pilgrims and monks—and an abbot!—rushing out the church doors. I sighed. "I wish I'd been there."

"You silly goose: you were. When you came flopping out . . ." His voice caught, and he looked away.

"So you got back the relics," I said, simply.

"'Twas not the relics that concerned me. . . ." He stared at the marshes lining the road, the air dark with insects. "When I lived here, this land was all villas."

"Wasn't it muddy?"

He snorted. "We drained it. We turned this wasteland into gardens and homes. 'Twas beautiful, Boy. But then the barbarians came and the ditches clogged, and no one knew how to drain them." He spat. "Barbarians know *nothing*."

A howl in the distance . . . wolves.

Even Secundus shivered. "Nor did we tolerate *that*. . . . Behold, Boy, the grand walls of Rome." For ahead stretched a high battered wall. "The boundary of the city."

"Did your people build that?" The wall looked to go on for miles.

"To keep out barbarians. Not that it worked. Now wolves prowl the city. Romans these days are more useless than dung."

We passed through the sagging gates, and oh, my disappointment, for the city looked no different from the wasteland outside. The road remained cracked and rutted, and trees grew through rotting roofs. I looked for wolves . . . but saw only shadows where they might hide.

We came to a structure so enormous that I could not see its far side. "That, Boy, was the grandest bath in Rome. Its library held more wisdom than the world today knows." He flipped to a page of his book: a drawing of a building with arches and statues and fountains, and a ceiling nigh as high as the sun.

"You drew that, milord?"

"I lived it. I drew it so I might remember . . ." He nodded to a vine-choked ruin. "There, I believe, was the villa of my dear friend Marius. He had a sculpture of Hercules wrestling a lion. It used to terrify Lucius. He'd stare and stare. . . ."

Lucius. Secundus's son.

"Flavia scolded that I'd give the boy nightmares. But that only happened once. He imagined the lion was outside our door. He cried out for me. Me—not Flavia. Not the nurse." He smiled. "I told him a lion would never attack us. I said, 'I'm too stringy to eat.' Then he asked, 'What about me?' A lawyer already. And I said, 'You're too small. You wouldn't fill one lion tooth.' And with that he rolled over and went back to sleep." Secundus gazed into space, his eyes a thousand years away.

"I am sorry, milord," I whispered. "I am sorry for your loss."

"For so long, I did not let myself hope. And now the memories come flooding back."

Memories flooded me as well: Sir Jacques tossing his son as the boy shrieked in glee. Sir Jacques laughing at my nonsense song, and scolding that I must eat . . .

Dusk darkened the sky. We passed houses packed with pilgrims, and church steps with monks doling out bread—not enough bread, for the pilgrims complained. We passed tents of folk left homeless by the earthquake. Women tended their cook fires right in the road, their children playing betwixt pilgrims' feet.

"Don't hunch, Boy," whispered Secundus. And later: "What are you doing?"

"I—I'm walking. Isn't this how folk walk?"

He laughed. "I don't think so."

So I tried harder . . . but how can one try to be normal? Normal is what somebody is.

We arrived at a vast square filled with pilgrims and tents. Straw sellers moved through the crowd hawking bedding. 'Twas a pity they couldn't hawk baths.

We entered the Mother of All the Churches, through doors as big as a barn. This building had suffered worse, even, than the church of Saint Paul, its roof also smashed to naught by the horrible earthquake. The walls bore black streaks where flames had clawed skyward, and the columns yet standing were charred black as the night.

"Milord, this is awful."

"Indeed. I had not anticipated such crowds." Brown-robed pilgrims packed the church. Pilgrims beyond counting lined up to worship, catching us in their midst, and pushing us forward.

Miraculously, the altar had not burned in the fire, and neither had the two heads. They lay upon the altar: the head of Saint Peter and the head of Saint Paul, each with pink wax cheeks and glass eyes and gray hair (Saint Peter) and a red beard and bald pate (Saint Paul). The heads were so close that I almost could touch them—were it not for the thick bars protecting the altar.

"Hello, Saint Peter," I whispered. The blank glass eyes stared.

A monk poked an old woman. "Move along; you're blocking the line. Move, boy."

He did not call me hunchback! The washerwomen had folded me well.

So we were pushed along, Secundus and I, two corks in an ocean of pilgrims, and we made it back outside, past the doors as big as a barn.

Secundus found a quiet shadow, and sat with a sigh. "So many people."

"Yes, milord. But luckily you have a plan." However did those doors close?

"I did not expect such crowds."

"What does your book say?"

"My book says naught," he snapped. "I'm not a magician. I've my wits and my key—that is all."

We stared at the Mother of All the Churches, its blackened

columns holding up air. Peddlers sold wine and bread and roasted meats, and pilgrims sang songs both pious and naughty, and a racket of birds heralded nightfall.

"Perhaps you could get a dog to steal us the head," Secundus suggested.

"I could not! Besides, a dog couldn't reach it."

"Hmph. Never mind."

Eat, eat! shrieked the birds. *To nest—to nest!*

Pilgrims passed, whispering as they looked at me. No signs of protection, but still . . .

"Don't hunch," said Secundus.

"But they're staring." Oh, I did not like that sensation. My skin prickled.

"They're not staring, they're looking." Secundus shut his eyes. "They've been stuck in some flea-bitten village since the day they were born. This is their one chance for adventure." He snorted. "Looking at us . . . How in the name of heaven will we get that skull?"

"Do not lose faith. Saint Peter wants us to have it."

"He does, does he?"

"Of course." I patted the pack. "Or he wouldn't have given

us five of his relics."

A swallow swooped past: *Eat, eat! Nest, nest!*

Secundus sighed, eyes still closed. "You're right. We'll simply walk in and take it."

Night comes, it comes! the birds called.

I frowned, thinking. "Milord? I might have an idea."

28 ❖ Skull, the Sixth

Dawn broke. Above the blackened church, the night sky softened to rose.

Inside the church I stood, in a crowd of pilgrims. Secundus was somewhere outside. "Keep him safe," I murmured to the pack on my back. "And me, too," I added. "Please."

Around me pilgrims gossiped or prayed, and slowly we approached the altar. I squeezed my eyes shut, whispering words that were almost a prayer. *Show me,* I whispered. *I am a fledgling. Show me how to fly.* These words I sent up to the sky.

A voice reached my ears: *What, what? An earth crawler speaks!*
Another: *Look: A fledgling, a fledgling!*
Others joined in: *What, what? A fledging? No! No!*

Yes, yes! the voice answered. *Let us show him, friends. Come, friends. Let us show!*

I opened my eyes.

A swallow flew over me, skimming my curls. *Not so close,* I laughed. *We'll get caught.* I was so near to the altar that I almost could touch its bars—

A starling swooped by. *Only one?* asked I. *Surely Rome has more than one starling.*

Just wait! snapped the starling. *Just wait—you'll see.*

I was at the altar, the head of Saint Peter an arm's length away.

"Move along," droned the monk. "Move along, boy." And then: "Goodness me . . ."

"Look!" whispered a pilgrim, and another. "Look up!"

Show me, friends, I smiled. *Show me what happiness means.*

You see? You see? the starling chirped. A dozen starlings. More starlings than stars.

Swallows swooped through the sky. *Fledgling, fledgling! We fly! We fly!*

I see, I answered. *'Tis glorious.*

A flock of doves soared like a smooth gray cloud. Crows swooped, cawing: *Watch, fledgling, how tough we are!* Sparrows flew in their little jerks. *Any crumbs? Any crumbs?* they twittered to each other, their eyes searching, always searching. . . .

But 'twas the starlings that captured the morn. The morn, and the attention of every soul in that church. Up they swirled, filling the sky, and in a spiral they soared from one end of the church to the other. They billowed and whirled, a thick wave, a thin line. *Envy us, earth crawlers!* they chortled, spiraling around the black columns.

The pilgrims stared and gaped at them, and wonder marked every face.

All day I could watch the starlings. The starlings and swallows and sparrows and crows, the doves and larks, the geese arriving now, the swans with strong beats. The terns. Three hawks high above. Flying, they were, with their wings.

I had wings. . . .

You're a fool, I scolded myself, dragging my gaze down to the earth crawlers. *There is work to be done.* I looked about—I sensed eyes on me. But no one seemed to be watching. Even the monks gawked at the birds.

I slipped my hand forward, easing my arm betwixt the bars. *We fly, we fly!* the birds sang—

My fingers met the wax head, and something warm beneath the wax . . .

Watch! The starlings swooped, writing a poem across the heavens that only God could read.

The wax covered a fragment of bone—but the fragment came loose as I touched it. A fragment of skull it was—a fragment missing one tooth. Of course: the tooth rested in my pack, safe and warm.

See us, see us, cried the starlings—

A shriek from the far end of the church. "Thief!" screamed a man. "A thief's over here!"

Quickly I lifted the fragment of skull—did the monks see? No!—and pulled it between the bars. I dived between pilgrims.

"Thief!" screamed the voice. "The thief is beside me!"

The monks peered over the crowd, searching for the man who screamed *thief.*

"Thief!" bellowed the man, for his belly was filled with wine and bread, and his purse with Secundus's coins. Beggars are loud, yes, but bribed beggars are even louder. "He's right here!"

I burrowed between pilgrims' legs.

"Thief!" cried the monks, repeating the cry.

"Thief!" cried the pilgrims, shoving.

I ducked through the crowd. Everywhere pilgrims blocked me: pilgrims with boots, pilgrims with sandals, pilgrims with thick yellow nails. Pilgrims as broad as bulls, and skinny pilgrims standing together as close as the weaves of a basket. I wiggled and pushed and crawled. . . .

At last, at last, I reached the threshold. I dashed out of the church—past doors as big as a barn—into the square. The square almost as crowded, and busy with the business of pilgriming.

"Hurry!" cried Secundus, struggling with the great church doors, his face flushed. "You there," he called to a cobbler. "We must seal the church against thieves!"

"Thieves?" The cobbler jumped up from his bench. "I won't stand for thieving." He pushed, and Secundus pushed, and the great doors slammed shut.

With a show of bustle Secundus locked the doors with his key, ignoring the pounding inside. "Thank goodness—and thanks to you, good cobbler. Now the church is safe." Away he strode, leaning on his staff.

I followed. I followed him past the stalls of butchers and the stalls of bloodletters, past piles of horse muck swarming with flies, past ruins higher than trees. Above my head the starlings laughed. But the swallows were gone, and already the crows mobbed the hawks.

How brave the crows were, attacking—

Don't think about birds, I scolded myself.

Secundus drew to a halt. He mopped his brow, and gasped for air. "Well?"

Cautiously—no one must see!—I showed him the fragment.

"Ah," he exhaled. "Rib tooth thumb toe dust skull."

"Rib tooth thumb toe dust skull." I slipped the skull in my pack. "Now we only need home."

Secundus laughed as he set off. "*Tomb,* Boy. Not home. Forever you make that mistake. We need only reach the tomb of Saint Peter. Naught will thwart us now!" But his laughter turned to coughing, and he walked like a very old man.

I took his arm, and looked around, and looked behind us, and looked behind us again, and coaxed him to walk faster. Someone—I knew it—was watching.

29 ⦂ Brigands and Wolves

And so we trudged the broken road. Secundus stumbled, and I caught him.

He chuckled. "You saved me, Boy."

Dark, this road was, even in daylight. Overgrown. Again my skin prickled. . . .

"Do you hear?" he repeated. "You saved me. For a thousand years I thought only of my own pain. You reminded me what it means to be human."

I pondered his words. "You have saved me, too. Before I met you, people threw stones."

"Hmph. They threw stones because you hunched. You don't hunch anymore—"

A terrible sound hit my ears: wolves, howling in the distance!

"Hurry!" whispered Secundus.

"Hurry!" I said, at the same time.

But alas, my master could only plod.

We reached the crest of a hill, gasping . . . but gasping in awe as well as fright, for before us spread a valley filled with ruins, and beyond it a crowded, rickety, smoke-covered town. "All this," Secundus wheezed, "was once the great city of Rome. From here to the walls. A million people! Now it has barely enough souls to fill a church."

We descended, Secundus murmuring of palaces and courts and statues. I tried to shush him: he must save his breath, and the wolves might hear us. . . .

Howls reached us—closer. *Brothers! Sisters!* the wolves cried. *Blood kill!*

"Milord," I whispered, horrified, "I can understand them!"

"What do they say?" He saw my face. "Ah. Nothing good."

The howls turned to barks: *Brothers, sisters—to scent! A man! A small one!*

"Run, Boy!" Secundus pushed me.

"I cannot leave you—" *I'm so scared!*

The crashing of underbrush. *Sisters! Brothers! Blood kill!*

A yelp of surprise: *The small one—it speaks!*

A wolf burst onto the road—a huge white she-wolf. She crouched, blocking our way.

I froze. Secundus froze. I tried not to exhale.

She lunged at us, sniffing. *You're not human.*

I . . . I gulped. *I'm an angel. I think.*

"Are you talking to it?" Secundus whispered, not moving his mouth.

Silence! The wolf stepped closer. *What is that one?*

He's my master.

Is he kin?

Without warning, a sob caught in my throat. *Yes. He is all the family I have.*

The wolf stared at Secundus with her cold yellow eyes. . . .

She slipped back into the weeds. *Sisters,* she called. *Brothers. We hunt elsewhere.*

She was gone.

Clutching his chest, Secundus sat on a fallen column. His cheeks were gray, and his lips.

"That was right terrifying," I gasped.

"I am not sure . . . I can . . . continue."

"You must! We are so close. Rib tooth thumb toe dust skull—you should cross out the word *skull*!"

He did not take out his book, however, but stared into space. "What chance do I have. Me? In heaven?"

"Milord, you must have faith."

He snorted. "Delusion, more like it."

I shook him—that is how angry I was! "I know—I know as truly as I know the sun shines—that if we make it to the tomb, you will be saved, and I'll be saved, too."

"You? You don't need saving."

"I do. I must become a boy."

"What?" He blinked.

"I know Saint Peter will grant my prayer. We need only reach his tomb—"

A noise—

I sprang up. Secundus turned.

A figure climbed out of the brush—a small figure with bare feet and black hair and red ribbons. 'Twas the girl who called herself wicked! The girl who threw stones.

"Oh, no," I whispered.

She strolled to us, laughing. "You two almost got eaten! A

waste of my time that'd have been." She looked at Secundus. "I'll give you twenty florins for your servant and his pack."

With effort he stood. "Neither is for sale."

"I figured as much. What of a partnership? With that pack, the two of us could own this city."

He snorted. "The pack is worthless."

"Worthless, eh? Not if it holds the skull of Saint Peter." She chuckled as I flinched. "Oh, I watched you take it. Quite a trick that was with the birds. But then, you're an angel." She grinned. "Climbing out of Saint Paul's with wings on your back . . . and me thinking you were a girl."

"You are mad," Secundus told her. Gripping my elbow, he walked.

"I wouldn't travel that way," the girl called. "You're better off going with me."

Secundus's breath rasped, but his voice remained strong: "Ignore her."

"Fine," she called. "We'll just sell his feathers and tears . . . Imagine: angel tears! I could buy all the silk in Rome. . . ."

Step by step, Secundus walked through the wasteland. I walked beside him.

A flash of black as she darted past—

She blocked the road, knife in hand. "I told you: this way's not safe."

Secundus swung his staff, smacking her hand aside.

Oh, was I awed. Many times I'd seen my master brave, but never so brave as this, for I knew the effort it cost him.

The girl hissed a curse, but she ducked away, and spat at our feet as we passed. "You'll regret this!" She continued to shout, but I focused on holding Secundus for he swayed like a reed, and together we tramped past swamp-filled temples and enormous white marble buildings.

"I shan't offer again," the girl yelled.

We approached a fortress—a fortress that once had been a great arch covered in statues but was now topped with battlements, its great arch filled in.

Behind us, the girl whistled—

Figures emerged from the fortress. Swordsmen, and a sharp-faced man:

The steward!

"I told you this route was unsafe." The girl smirked at us. She held out her palm to the steward. "I brought them to you as I promised. Now pay me."

The steward turned to the swordsmen. "Kill her. Kill the pilgrim. Keep the servant."

The swordsmen lunged—without warning Secundus was knocked to the ground. He lay motionless, his hat in the dirt—

"Secundus!" I cried—

"Shut up," the girl hissed, her knife at my throat. "I've caught your prize bird!" she yelled to the steward. "Send off your men or I'll kill him. Then I'll gut you like the French pig you are."

I began to cry—I could not help it. We had been so close!

"Stop wasting your tears!" Her knife pricked my neck.

Help, thought I, helplessly.

The steward glared at the girl. His swordsmen stepped back. . . .

"Hold your ground!" he shouted at them.

Still the swordsmen backed away. With a clang, they dropped their weapons.

The steward stared at us, his face ashen. He stared past us.

The swordsmen turned and fled.

"Wolves!" the steward screamed. He ran.

The girl spun—

A pack of wolves pounded toward us. The white wolf leaped for me—

The wolf sank her teeth into the girl's wrist, wrenching her sideways.

I stumbled away—

Secundus stirred.

"Milord!" I crawled to him.

The steward ran—oh, he ran fast. Three wolves behind him . . .

The white wolf tossed the girl to the ground. *Blood kill! I shall rip out her throat—*

No! I cried.

The wolf stared at me, her claws on the girl's neck. *You called for help.*

I know. I shook Secundus. "Wake, milord, please." Blood ran from a wound on his forehead.

She would not be missed, the wolf growled.

Perhaps not. But 'tis enough that you saved me. I gathered Secundus's hat and staff. "Come, milord. Can you walk, do you think?"

"Ah, my head hurts." Secundus struggled to sit.

"We haven't much farther. . . ." I looked up to the wolf: *Thank you—*

But the white wolf was gone.

The girl lay in the dirt. Disbelief filled her face. Disbelief, and something more: fear. "That beast was going to kill me," she whispered.

I turned to Secundus. "Lean on me. . . ."

She said something I could not make out. "Answer me!" she shouted.

"Answer you what?" I hadn't time for her chatter.

"You stopped that wolf—I know you did. Why?"

"Because I am good." I adjusted Secundus's arm on my shoulder. "One step—well done." I could sense the girl's eyes on me, but I ignored her. "You are doing brilliantly, milord . . ."

I had not killed her, no. And the girl was too feared to follow me, I could tell. But she'd almost killed me. She'd stalked me all the way across Rome. Stalked me like I was prey . . .

Oh, I needed to reach the tomb of Saint Peter. Then I never again would know fear. At the tomb of Saint Peter, my troubles would end.

30 ∵ Tomb, the Seventh

On we plodded. Chipped columns rose between weeds. Buildings lay in pieces, or stood with their windows barricaded by rubble. Like termites, Romans now were.

"This once was the Forum." Secundus mopped at the blood on his forehead. "Now it's buried by a thousand years of ashes and filth." He stared at a cow pat.

I put my arm around his waist. "Come, milord."

Still we walked. I pleaded for help from pilgrims camping in this wasteland, and from Romans living amid collapsed houses. But as one they ignored us.

The smells worsened: sweat and piss pots and pigs. We were in the city itself now, cracked towers looming over cramped streets. Secundus peered around, each breath wracking his frame. "I feel," he gasped, "a thousand years old. . . ."

"Move, I say!" A well-fed pilgrim rode a donkey toward us. The pilgrim's rings twinkled in the sunshine as he beat the donkey's flanks.

Oh, donkey, I cried. *How awful it is that he whips you.*

The donkey's ears pricked. *A talker—haw!* His nose curled. *Your man stinks of farts.*

"Move, you stupid beast!" The pilgrim hit his mount.

"Excuse me," I tried, "but perhaps if you did not beat him—"

"'Tis not your business!"

I'm so sorry, I said to the donkey. On I toiled, Secundus leaning on me, his forehead oozing.

A mob pressed around a wheelbarrow with a leaky barrel of wine, men elbowing each other, cups in hand. We edged past this mob, barely, but the gold-ringed pilgrim could not. His shouts rose over the hubbub: "Make way, I say!"

Secundus looked about, frowning. "Ah, Boy, the city is so different. . . ."

"I say!" screamed the gold-ringed pilgrim.

I looked back—just in time to see the donkey toss the

pilgrim off his back. *Haw!* declared the donkey. *I've better humans to carry.* He kicked his hooves and scrambled through the mob as though the men were no more than boulders. He trotted up to Secundus. *Get on me, you stinker.*

Oh, donkey, I cried—

Haw! I hate manners. And then, as Secundus hauled himself into the saddle: *Your master sits like a bagful of beans.*

Thank you, I whispered to Saint Peter. This donkey was nigh a miracle.

Off we set, the donkey and Secundus and I. Secundus's breathing eased, and his color improved. . . .

Ahead of us, metal glinted above the crowd: pikes. Soldiers approached!

The donkey eyed me: *What's wrong, you? You're panting.*

What if the soldiers were hunting for us? I hunched—I should not hunch—

"Make way," A soldier cried. He peered at Secundus. "Is that blood?" His horse eyed us—

Haw! snarled the donkey. *Look elsewhere, you overfed pony.*

The horse jerked, almost unsaddling the soldier. Distracted, the soldier rode on.

Thank you, donkey, I breathed.

Haw. I hate show-offs.

One by one the soldiers passed us, their horses shying from the donkey's teeth.

Secundus blinked. "Are those . . . horsemen?" He swayed.

"Do not worry. We are safe." Safe, at least, for the moment.

Still the crowds grew: porters bearing charcoal and flour and hay. Errand boys. Noblemen. Rag pickers. Jugglers and acrobats. Nuns. Innkeepers bawling their fees. And pilgrims everywhere, pushing.

A stench of wet and rot and sewage. "Ah," sighed Secundus. "The river."

We crossed a bridge crammed with food stalls and shrines. *Step aside!* cried the donkey, gleefully nipping at pilgrims.

And then we were there. At the steps of the church of the tomb of Saint Peter. The biggest church in all the world, and the most important—so important that pilgrims climbed the steps on their knees. Businesses crowded these steps: money changers with benches of coins, merchants displaying bolts of fine silk, spice dealers with sacks of rare spices, tooth pullers wielding pliers . . .

"I saw this when first 'twas built." Secundus gazed at the church. "The steps . . . we called them the steps to paradise."

Up we climbed, the donkey's hooves ringing on the marble. I marveled at the church's great bronze gates, and the masses of pilgrims—more pilgrims and merchants than ever I'd seen.

We reached the threshold. A stout priest blocked our path. "Here now, you can't bring a donkey inside."

I bit back a cry of frustration. "Please, Father. Please help us."

"I'd like to, but . . ." He stared at Secundus. "Why, this one's bleeding."

I clasped his hands. "We've come so far! Please, Father—we must get to the tomb!"

"Ah, you look so desperate . . ." The priest scratched his jaw. "How tame is this creature?"

"He is always behaved, Father. See?" *Please, donkey. Give me a kiss.*

The donkey twitched his ears . . . but he gave my fingers a nibble, and rubbed against me.

"You won't be long, will you?"

"No, Father!" I hugged him, and nigh skipped across the threshold. We were inside the church of the tomb of Saint Peter! I could scarce shut my mouth, I was so awed. A thousand candles burned. The sound of hymns and prayers mingled with the scents of incense and beeswax. Even Secundus gaped.

The donkey's hooves slipped on the marble floor. *Haw, 'tis too loud for me.*

I am sorry, donkey. You are so kind to carry—

Haw. More blather.

Secundus reached for me. "We did it, Boy."

"Yes, milord." I squeezed his scarred hand. "Soon you will be in heaven."

"And you will be a boy." He managed a chuckle. "Until you're an angel again."

"You are right." I blinked back tears. "Perhaps we shall meet in paradise."

"I should . . . like that." He wiped his fever-bright eyes, and gestured to a staircase beneath the altar. "Down there is the tomb."

I coaxed the donkey down the steps. *How much longer?* he asked as we shuffled along a crowded passageway.

Not long, I think— "Milord? Are you ready?"

He smiled. "Yes, Lucius."

"I am not—" How fine for him to think of his son. Soon enough he would see him!

We rounded a curve. "The tomb!" cried pilgrims, kneeling at a gate in the passageway's wall. They reached out their hands: "The tomb!"

A silk-robed clergyman hauled up the pilgrims. "You've seen enough. Move along."

Closer we drew, closer to this gate. Suddenly I realized: "Milord, the tomb is too far away! We can't touch it!"

Secundus blinked. "Yes . . . The gate . . . is locked. . . ."

Behind us, pilgrims pushed and jostled—

The donkey's ears twitched. *Haw! 'Tis too loud!*

"Milord, what is your plan?"

"Plan? We must open . . ." He tried to focus on his book. "I can't find . . . the page. . . ."

"Move along!" the clergyman bawled.

What's wrong? cried the donkey. *You're panting again!*

The clergyman caught sight of the donkey. "A beast? In my church?"

Beast, is it? Haw! The donkey bared his teeth.

"Come, milord." I helped Secundus dismount. We'd get as close as we could.

"Shoo!" cried the clergyman, flapping his hands.

Don't flap at me! brayed the donkey, kicking.

Secundus reached for the gate. "Lucius . . . Flavia . . ."

"Run!" shouted the pilgrims. "The donkey's gone mad!" They shoved each other, panicking.

"Stop shouting!" shouted the clergyman.

Secundus reached between the bars toward the tomb out of reach.

"Shoo, you asinine creature!" The clergyman slapped the donkey's nose—

How rude! The donkey snapped his teeth—and ripped off the clergyman's robe! *Never insult a donkey!* He galloped down the passageway, the fine silk robe flapping. *Haw!*

The clergyman chased him, clad only in his undershirt,

followed by the rest of the pilgrims.

"The Lord," murmured Secundus, "works in . . . mysterious ways."

Silence. The passageway stood empty. "Quick, milord! The key!"

"The key? Ah . . ." He fumbled at his robe. "My fingers . . ."

"I have it, milord." Oh, the key stank. But it slipped into the lock. The gate opened.

The tomb lay before us.

"Take my arm." Three strides we'd need, perhaps, to reach it.

"The tomb . . ." Secundus breathed. "Seven . . . relics . . . I must . . . gather. . . ."

"Milord!" I tore at the cords on my chest. "Rib tooth thumb toe dust skull home—no!" I laughed. "Tomb, not home. I always get the last one wrong."

"Perhaps 'tis not the tomb you seek." He smiled. "Goodbye, angel. I love you."

"I love you, too, milord. For always."

He took the pack of Saint Peter. He reached—I reached—

We touched the tomb wall.

I shivered in delight. How warm it felt . . .

"What are you doing? Get *out* of there!" The clergyman charged toward us!

I spun to look—I spun back—

On the floor lay a tatter of brown pilgrim cloth, and dust, and a few withered bones. Bones that looked to be one thousand years old.

Secundus was gone.

31 ⁘ Boyhood

"Off with you!" screeched the clergyman, pounding toward me.

"The tomb is open!" shouted pilgrims, rushing the gate.

"Saint Peter," I prayed, my hands on the tomb, "please make me a—"

The clergyman grabbed me. "Don't touch that! Where'd the tall pilgrim go?" He dragged me through the pilgrims, snapping that everyone must leave at once.

"Saint Peter!" I cried. "Secundus!" But I did not struggle much, for I could yet feel wings beneath my tunic, and I feared that the clergyman would feel them, too.

So I was yanked away, the clergyman bawling that I was a thief, and two burly pilgrims carried me through the church whilst everyone glared. How grief filled me! I peered up through the windows to the blue sky beyond. Secundus was in heaven—he accomplished his quest! But oh, I missed him. "Help me, Secundus," I whispered. "Help me, now that you are in paradise."

But no help came. The two burly pilgrims kept their grip on my arms, and the crowd hissed its displeasure.

They dumped me at the church gates. "Be thankful you're not suffering worse," snapped one, brushing dust from his hands.

"You!" A stout priest strode over—the priest who had allowed in the donkey. He gestured down the steps. "Look!"

I looked down at the sellers of books and badges and cloths and fruit . . . but the fruit sellers' baskets were toppled, with apples and apricots everywhere, and bunches of grapes sprawled like drunkards. . . .

"Your donkey did that!" cried the priest.

"I'm sorry, but—" I turned back. I must reach the tomb—

"Go!" cried the priest, balling his fists. "Go before I have you flogged!"

So I ran. I ran past the baskets and pilgrims and merchants, for I did not want to be flogged!

I ran till I found myself in a rank alleyway with a broken-down staircase, and no one in sight but a skinny brown dog.

I tucked myself beneath the stair. Slowly I reached . . .

My heart sank. I still had wings, most definitely. Folded, yes, but wings.

I had made it to Rome. I'd touched the very tomb of Saint Peter! Yet still I was not a boy. I must finish my prayer at the tomb . . . but how?

A woman appeared, her face as wrinkled as an old apple. "What are you up to?"

"I'm sorry, I was resting—"

"Away with you, boy!" She flapped her apron—so like Cook that I jumped. Cook who flapped her apron when she scolded me for not working.

The old woman creaked up the stairs. "Useless boy. You'll steal my hens, I'm sure. . . ." She slammed the door behind her.

I don't steal hens, I wanted to say. I did not speak, however. But neither did I move, for I had nowhere to go. *Hello,* I greeted the skinny brown dog.

The dog scratched her neck.

Dog? I called. How strange that she did not answer. . . .

Three swallows swooped through the alley. *Eat, eat,* they cried. How they soared! Watching them, my wings prickled—

Stop, wings! I scolded myself.

And then . . . a voice came to me:

Why?

I jumped: "Secundus!"

But the voice did not come from the alley. It came from inside my head. *Why?* asked the voice in that tone I knew—the tone Secundus used to turn my mind into knots and make me think wrong was right. Although sometimes wrong was actually right. . . . *Why can't your wings move?* asked the voice.

Because—oh, 'twas important how I answered. *Because folk will see I'm an angel.*

The brown dog paused her scratching. *Eh?* said she. *Did somebody speak?*

Above me the door slammed open: the old woman emptying a piss pot. "Away, boy, I said!" She slammed the door shut.

Did somebody speak? the dog repeated. With effort she stood. Her tail wagged.

I sat with a plop, for I had no strength to stand. My head spun with notions and thoughts. . . .

The old woman called me a boy! came one thought. *She didn't call me hunchback or monster.* The pilgrims in Saint Peter had glared, yes. But none made the sign of protection. I might have wings, but thanks to the washerwomen, my tunic lay smooth on my back. My hump was right gone.

A second thought: *Oh, 'tis grand to speak to creatures.*

A third: *My, but piss stinks!* Which I'd thought before, as does anyone who visits a city, but at this moment it struck me. If I were a boy, I'd have to piss. And eat, and drink, and squat—every day! What a tremendous waste of time. What a stench. Perhaps being a boy had its drawbacks.

My fourth thought was the face of Saint Peter, frowning at me over his beard. *Are you an angel,* he had asked, *or a boy?* Right now I did not know the answer!

And my last thought, loudest of all, was a word. The word *fly.*

The dog plodded over.

I scratched her ears. *What am I, dog? An angel, or a boy?*

Eh? The dog panted. *What's the question again?*

You are both, came a voice—the voice in my head. The voice that'd been taught by Secundus. *You are a boy to folk who would harm you. But in your heart, you're an angel.*

Above my head, the door slammed again: the old woman snapping a dust cloth. "No help at all . . ." So like Cook: muttering. Scolding. Always putting others to work. Cook had not even called for a priest. She'd had time to scurry, yes, during the pestilence, but not time enough to save the soul of milady—

Oh. I realized, at last, the truth:

Cook hadn't time to be good. She was too busy tending the sick. Too busy keeping the manor alive.

Dazed, I rose to my feet. Under my tunic, my wings shifted, folding themselves—

My wings. I had wings.

Did it matter if I lacked parts? Not if I remained clothed!

The old woman struggled down the stairs with a basket of linens. "Ne'er-do-wells, the lot of them . . ."

I squared my shoulders. I could no longer hide. "Excuse me. Might I help?"

She scowled at me. "You'll not steal this, you naughty boy!"

"I won't, I promise. But I could carry the basket for you."

Her wrinkled-apple face tightened. "I can't pay you."

"Of course not." Gently I took the basket from her grip.

The dog followed us, wagging her tail.

"Why are you doing this?" the old woman snapped.

Because a saint told me to, I wanted to say. *Because inside I'm an angel, and angels are good.* "Because there is work. I like helping."

Her scowl shifted, a little. "Well." She tucked a hair under her cap. "'Tis the least you can do." So like Cook . . .

I grinned. There was gratitude there somewhere, if you had the sense to sniff it out.

Three swallows swooped down the alley. *Fledgling! Fledgling! Come fly! Come fly!*

My wings prickled, aching to open . . . That night on the ship when I stretched them, the air warm all around my feathers . . .

"You're walking too fast. I'm not a spring chicken, you know."

I dragged my eyes earthward. "My apologies."

She grunted. "For a boy, you're not too ill-mannered . . . you have curls like an angel."

I grinned—I could not help it. "So I've been told." I nodded to the basket. "Where would you like me to take this?"

"Don't be so impatient. And get away, you." She flapped her apron at the dog.

What? asked the dog. *What'd I do?*

Nothing, dog... "She's fine, I'm sure. Perhaps you might have a bone?"

"A bone? For a stray?" The old woman grimaced—no, wait. A hint of a smile.

There's a bone in your future, I whispered to the dog.

The dog's ears perked up. *A bone? What's future?*

And so I strolled at the old woman's pace, the basket on my hip, the dog wagging behind us. The sun warmed my curls (curls like an angel!), and my bare dirty toes, and the tunic that covered my wings.

Swallows swooped past, their wings brushing my ears. *You've feathers, fledgling! Come fly!*

I shall, I answered. *But not yet. There is work.* "There is work...."

The woman's face softened as she watched the swallows lift and dive, and for a moment her eyes shone like a child's. "What's that, boy?"

"Something a wise man once told me." Saint Paul, in fact. "He said there was work to be done." And joy in the labor. Such joy, if you knew how to find it.

32 ❖ Rib Tooth Thumb Toe Dust Skull Home

How small the manor looked, sitting on its hill. The manor that had once been my world . . .

I passed an empty hut with a makeshift door. For a moment my heart beat: had pestilence returned? But a pig lolled in the pigsty, which reassured me. The pigsty fence was well tended. Someone took care of this pig.

Hello, pig.

I'm hungry, complained the pig.

You're always hungry. I laughed, for hunger is the nature of pigs. *Enjoy this sunshine.*

On I walked. The pig would not know sunshine much longer. Autumn meant harvest, and soon enough the pig would become sausage and hams. Poor pig . . . though the creature seemed content enough, and the September sun was fine.

In the distance stood the orchard. Last March the trees had been crowded with too many branches, but now fat apples dangled from the pruned limbs. The trees were as well cared for as the pig.

I am as different as those trees. I smiled, smoothing my tunic. Between my shoulders lay my well-folded wings. Each night I stretched them, feeling the air, and then settled them like two hands at prayer. *Not yet, wings,* I promised. *But soon.*

My toes met the path up the hill, each pebble as familiar as teeth. *Hello, manor—*

Boy, Boy! cried the dogs. *Boy, Boy, you are back, you are back!* They sniffed my hands and my hose. *You smell different, Boy, Boy! You smell of . . .*

I smell like an angel. I smiled. *I smell of Saint Peter and birds and two months' walking. I smell of a girl I returned to her mother, and the lost chicken I found, and the hay I helped cut—*

Hrmm, said the dogs, *too much words! Come on!*

And so I entered the courtyard—the courtyard of the manor of Sir Jacques.

Pots of thyme framed the kitchen door; trays of grapes lay

drying to raisins. I could not resist a glance at the cowshed. All the folk I met on my homeward journey had liked me. They'd shared their stories and homes and directions, and all of them had called me a boy. . . .

Stand up, my mind scolded. *If you slump like a monster, then so you'll be treated.*

A voice from the threshing room: "I said to sweep, you louse brain! Did you turn the cheeses? I thought not." Cook strode outside. "Tell the cooper I'll pay him once I know his barrels hold wine." She scanned the courtyard. . . .

Her eyes returned, taking me in. My straight back. My calm face. "You!" she snapped. "I thought you'd run off."

"Hello, milady. I took your cup to Saint-Peter's-Step as I promised. I prayed for you—"

"I've no time for chitchat. Tell your pilgrim he ruined my herdsman."

Ox? I turned to the dogs: *What happened to Ox?*

They danced round: *Did you not hear, Boy, Boy? He stomped away shouting!*

"Ox is gone?" The words fell out of my mouth.

"Went off to preach, the dimwit. Right before planting, too."

Ox a preacher? I could not imagine. Although preachers are loud and fierce, and Ox was both of those twice over.

I pictured Ox standing before a church, giving listeners the fear he'd once given me . . . Secundus must have filled him right full of hell's terrors! The strong didn't stand a chance, not with Ox protecting the weak.

Cook sniffed. "The goats have gone wild without you. You'll have a fine time tracking them down." She strode away. "Someone get the kittens out of the milk house. And check on the harvest! They'll ruin those grapes, I just know it. Where is that salt? I'll weigh it myself—I'm sure we've been robbed. . . ."

The dogs nuzzled my hands. *She scares us, Boy, Boy.*

I patted them. *She should. But she sees that you're fed.* I smiled. I was still the goatherd! What a relief that was.

I looked around. I had another soul to greet. . . .

There he sat. The sun caught the dent in his head, and the line of drool on his jaw.

Softly I approached. The dogs nuzzled his curled hands, hoping yet for a pat.

I knelt before him. "Hello, Sir Jacques."

He stared past me, his mouth agape.

Hello, milord. I spoke with my mind, as I speak to all creatures.

From somewhere within his broken skull, he answered. *Hello, Boy. My, you have grown.*

I smiled. *Yes, milord. I'm an angel, it seems.*

An angel? How grand. Do you . . . know where my wife is? I can't seem to find her.

I blinked back tears. *I am sorry, milord. She awaits you in heaven.*

Sir Jacques trembled, reaching—

I clasped his hands. How I used to marvel at his hands, the palms as calloused as tree bark. Now his skin was so soft . . . "Shh."

You were always so good. Help me, Boy.

I must! I was an angel! But how?

A notion came to me. *I am thinking of a place. See if you can see it with me.* In my head, I thought of a broad marble staircase. The steps to paradise . . .

Step by step, I climbed. Beside me—in my head—Sir Jacques crept. Weakly, for he had not walked in years. With both my arms I held him up. *Come, milord. I have someone to show you.*

We approached the bronze gates.

Saint Peter, I called. *Please help us.*

The gates cracked open. A figure stepped out—a pretty woman in a cream-colored gown, a baby in her arms. A shy little boy clung to her skirts, and a girl old enough to toddle.

"Greetings, Boy," milady smiled. "How fine to see you again." She reached to the bent man beside me. "Hello, my love."

Sir Jacques gripped my hand. *Can it be?* Tears ran down his face.

With great effort he stepped . . .

His hands uncurled. The dent in his skull disappeared. He lifted his children in his great strong arms, and he hugged milady, beaming. . . . "Thank you, Boy," he whispered.

"They are here, milord. They await you."

The vision ended. I was kneeling in the courtyard, Sir Jacques's hands in mine. His blank eyes stared . . . but a faint smile lifted his lips. *Thank you, Boy.*

And thank you, for your kindness to me, all of my life. I stood. *Stay with him,* I said to the dogs. *He needs you.*

Of course, Boy, Boy. They rested their heads in his lap, and curled at his feet.

I left the courtyard. How lovely paradise had been! How pretty milady. Someday I would meet her again, and the children. Someday I would join Secundus, and thank him for saving me.

But not yet. There was work to be done. Work . . . and something else, too.

I descended the hillside swarming with folk cutting grapes. I crossed the road—the road Secundus had walked six months before, his palm scarred from the rib of Saint Peter—

A thunder of hoofbeats. The goats! *Bah!* they cried. *Where have you been?* They bleated with joy, and leaped about almost like dogs. *You were gone an awfully long time!* The kids butted one another in glee.

Hello, goats! I've missed you—you've no idea.

Together we strolled to the orchard. *Why did you leave?* the goats demanded.

Well. I pondered. *I was on a quest. I had to find home.*

Home? Bah. They tossed their heads. *Home is here.*

I chuckled. *It took time to learn that.* I looked back at the manor, every soul busy at harvest, Cook bawling instructions. Whatever would we do without her? *It took time to find me.*

We arrived at the orchard so well pruned. Cook's doing,

no doubt. We came to the tree—the tree I climbed the day I met Secundus. How often I had dreamed of this moment. Each night as I stretched my wings, I'd think of the place I must start from. The tree that had once seemed so high, and the view from its top so vast. How vast my horizons were now.

Apples! cried the goats. *Feed us! Yum!*

You've food enough, you greedy creatures. I laughed. I slipped off my tunic, and tied it around my waist.

I looked around once more: no one could see me.

With a sigh of delight, I stretched out my wings. The September sun caught the white, the blue. Rich red. Flecks of gold. Oh, my wings had been patient.

I peered through the apple-filled branches to the blue autumn sky. I had climbed this tree in March, I had. With great effort I'd reached the top branch and I'd jumped, just to relish the feeling of flying.

But that was six months past.

Bah! The goats pranced. *Will you climb, Boy? Will you climb?*

I patted them, enjoying the breeze on my feathers. *I don't need to.*

I spread my wings, and I flew.

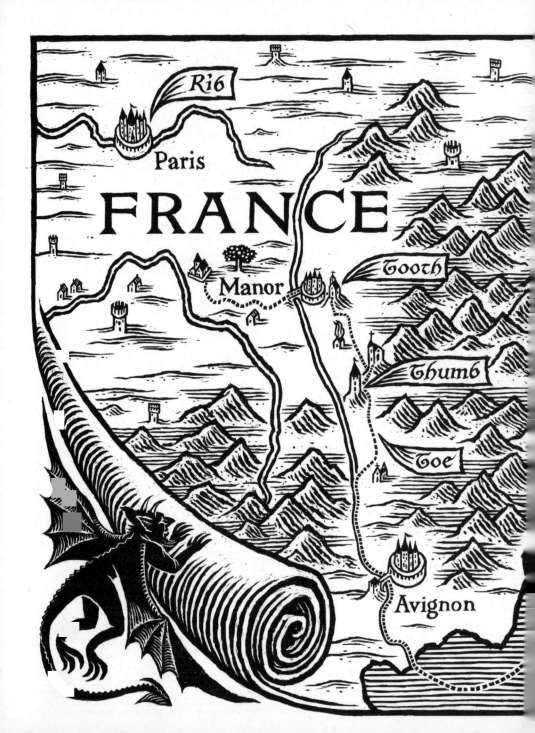

Author's Note

The Book of Boy is set during the Holy Year of 1350, when hundreds of thousands of Christians pilgrimed to the city of Rome. It was not an easy time. Bubonic plague had recently killed a third of the population of Europe. War touched England, France, Germany, Italy, Holland, and Spain; bands of unpaid soldiers held entire cities hostage. Starvation threatened, always, for food was hard to grow and even harder to transport.

Rome suffered especially. The pope had left the city early in the 1300s for the French city of Avignon; with his departure, the city lost its government and most of its wealth. In the 1340s, a bloody civil war destroyed many of Rome's buildings and families. Then came the earthquake of September 1349.

The poet Petrarch, visiting for the Holy Year, wrote:

> The houses are overthrown, the walls come to the ground, the temples fall, the sanctuaries perish, the laws are trodden underfoot. . . . The mother of all the churches stands without a roof and exposed to wind and rain. The holy dwellings of Saint Peter and Saint Paul totter. . . .

A later visitor reported wolves howling outside his door at night. Pilgrims in that Holy Year traveled in bands as protection from brigands, and slept four to a bed when they could find beds at all—or find food. They journeyed to both the tomb of Saint Peter and the grave of Saint Paul because, they believed, the saints' bodies were split between the two churches. They journeyed as well to the Mother of All the Churches, marveling at the saints' lifelike wax heads.

As *The Book of Boy* makes clear, relics in the Middle Ages were important to health, trade, and fame. Kings traveled with their relic collections, displaying them to prove their own power. Cities and monasteries stole one another's relics, and boasted publicly that they'd done so. Readers today might be disturbed or amused by all this attention paid to bits of bone and cloth. But modern halls of fame are filled with used guitar picks, sweaty jerseys, and cracked leather balls—not so different from the relics that pilgrims sought a thousand years ago.

Visitors to the church of Saint Paul in Rome can still see a hole in the coffin lid—the hole through which pilgrims once lowered cloth strips; the church also has an extraordinary collection of coins left by pilgrims over the centuries. In the 1940s, archeologists working in the church of Saint Peter discovered an ancient tomb beneath the floor, and within this tomb the actual bones of Peter.[1] The head of Saint Peter still resides at the Mother of All the Churches—a church better known today as Saint John Lateran. The skull sits in a gold vessel beside the head of Saint Paul, high above the altar, safe behind thick gilded bars.

---

[1] Which is to say, the bones of a man Saint Peter's age and build who died around the time of Saint Peter, and who had the name Peter (or *Petrus* in Latin).